D0961336

The Lost Diaries of
Adrian Mole, 1999–2001

By the same author

NOVELS
The Secret Diary of Adrian Mole Aged 13¾
The Growing Pains of Adrian Mole
Rebuilding Coventry
True Confessions of Adrian Albert Mole,
    Margaret Hilda Roberts and Susan Lilian Townsend
Adrian Mole: From Minor to Major
The Queen and I
Adrian Mole: The Wilderness Years
Ghost Children
Adrian Mole: The Cappuccino Years
Public Confessions of a Middle-aged Woman Aged 55¾
Number Ten
Adrian Mole and the Weapons of Mass Destruction
Queen Camilla

PLAYS
Womberang
The Ghost of Daniel Lambert
Dayroom
Captain Christmas and the Evil Adults
Bazaar and Rummage
The Great Celestial Cow
Disneyland It Ain't
The Queen and I

SCREENPLAYS
The Secret Diary of Adrian Mole
The Growing Pains of Adrian Mole
The Refuge
Adios

The Lost Diaries of Adrian Mole, 1999-2001

Sue Townsend

MICHAEL JOSEPH
an imprint of
PENGUIN BOOKS

MICHAEL JOSEPH

Published by the Penguin Group
Penguin Books Ltd, 80 Strand, London WC2R ORL, England
Penguin Group (USA) Inc., 375 Hudson Street, New York, New York 10014, USA
Penguin Group (Canada), 90 Eglinton Avenue East, Suite 700, Toronto, Ontario, Canada M4P 2Y3
(a division of Pearson Penguin Canada Inc.)
Penguin Ireland, 25 St Stephen's Green, Dublin 2, Ireland
(a division of Penguin Books Ltd)
Penguin Group (Australia), 250 Camberwell Road, Camberwell, Victoria 3124, Australia
(a division of Pearson Australia Group Pty Ltd)
Penguin Books India Pvt Ltd, 11 Community Centre, Panchsheel Park, New Delhi – 110 017, India
Penguin Group (NZ), 67 Apollo Drive, Rosedale, North Shore 0632, New Zealand
(a division of Pearson New Zealand Ltd)
Penguin Books (South Africa) (Pty) Ltd, 24 Sturdee Avenue, Rosebank, Johannesburg 2196, South Africa

Penguin Books Ltd, Registered Offices: 80 Strand, London WC2R ORL, England

www.penguin.com

First published 2008
3

Copyright © Lily Broadway Productions Ltd, 2008

The moral right of the author has been asserted

Content first published in the *Guardian* between 1999 and 2001

All rights reserved.
Without limiting the rights under copyright
reserved above, no part of this publication may be
reproduced, stored in or introduced into a retrieval system,
or transmitted, in any form or by any means (electronic, mechanical,
photocopying, recording or otherwise), without the prior
written permission of both the copyright owner and
the above publisher of this book

Set in 13/16 pt Minion
Typeset by Rowland Phototypesetting Ltd, Bury St Edmunds, Suffolk
Printed in Great Britain by Clays Ltd, St Ives plc

A CIP catalogue record for this book is available from the British Library

Hardback ISBN: 978–0–718–15489–9
Trade Paperback ISBN: 978–0–718–15490–5

www.greenpenguin.co.uk

Mixed Sources
Product group from well-managed
forests and other controlled sources
www.fsc.org Cert no. SA-COC-1592
© 1996 Forest Stewardship Council

Penguin Books is committed to a sustainable future
for our business, our readers and our planet.
The book in your hands is made from paper
certified by the Forest Stewardship Council.

This book is dedicated to babies of my acquaintance, in alphabetical order: Ava, Halle, Layla, Logan, Luca, Lyla, Marcus, Max, Mia, Michael and Paris

Acknowledgements

Acknowledgements

Love and thanks to Bailey Townsend for her invaluable help.

Foreword

These diaries were lost when I moved from my modest council estate home back to my parents' equally modest home in Ashby de la Zouch.

After the events of Saturday, 24 November 2001, when I was dragged out of my bed at 4 a.m. by an over-enthusiastic policeman citing David Blunkett's anti-terrorism laws, I could no longer return home.

My neighbours informed me that after I had been taken away to be questioned, people in white forensic suits took away every piece of paper in large sacks. Every floorboard was pulled up, plaster was taken off the walls, and the garden was dug and soil removed for examination.

After my release I asked for my 1999–2001 diaries, but was told that the police were hanging on to them should any charges be brought against me, Mohammed and his brother, Imran. Then last week I answered the door of the renovated pigsty where I now live to find a policeman holding my diaries, which were inside a transparent plastic bag.

He said, 'I think these belong to you, sir.'

I examined them and said, not without a hint of sarcasm, 'So I'm no longer under suspicion, am I? I'm not going to be snatched from my bed and flown on a rendition flight to be water-boarded in Turkey, then?'

The policeman said, extremely sarcastically, 'Oh, did we forget to tell you that you'd been cleared, sir? I do hope you haven't been tossing and turning in your bed at night, sir. We were closing the old police station down and we found these in the evidence store.' He handed the bag over to me. I said a curt thank-you and closed the door on him. On rereading my diary entries, I am struck by the melancholy tone of the majority of them. I do not seem to be able to find lasting love and my writing career remains but a dream.

I am now living with my wife, Daisy, and my four-year-old daughter, Gracie, in the aforementioned pigsty in a village called Mangold Parva in the Leicestershire countryside. I wish that I could relate that I have found happiness and contentment in my rural retreat but, alas, I cannot – but that is another story.

I remain, dear reader, your most humble and obedient servant.

Adrian Albert Mole.

P.S. These diary entries have appeared in the

Guardian previously, having been hi-jacked by a woman fraudster called Sue Townsend. She has made quite a lucrative living passing herself off as me. I know where she lives – I have been to her house and rung her doorbell but she refuses to come to the door. Once I saw her through the front window. She was a large shape sitting in the corner of a gloomy room swigging from what looked liked a bottle of Stolichnaya. Her garden is overgrown and her house is in disrepair – she has obviously fallen on bad times. I can't say I'm sorry. She has been a parasite on my literary career for too long.

1999

Friday, November 26, 1999, 2.30 p.m.
Wisteria Walk, Ashby de la Zouch, Leicestershire

I have not kept a diary since the fire destroyed my house, furniture, clothes, books and life savings. The arsonist, Eleanor Flood, is residing in a secure unit, where she is doing an MA. Her dissertation is entitled 'The Phoenix – Myth Or Metaphor?' I know, because she writes to me occasionally.

I have protested to the authorities, but they are powerless to stop her letters, which are obviously being smuggled out by a corrupt prison guard. As I lie in bed at night, listening to the breathing of my sons. William, 7, and Glenn, 13, in their bunk-beds only inches away from my head, I often think of Eleanor Flood, and envy her. At least she has a room of her own, and time in which to think and write.

11 p.m.
Took the boys to watch Santa abseiling down the side of Debenhams in Leicester tonight on his way to his grotto. William was enchanted by the sight of Santa

3

swinging from a climbing rope, but Glenn kept looking around anxiously at the crowd of onlookers. He said, 'If anybody from school sees me 'ere, I'm a dead man, Dad.'

The queue for the grotto was at least 70 deep. It snaked through Toys into Bed Linens and Small Electrical Appliances. To placate us, Debenhams played Sir Cliff Richard's rendition of the 'Lord's Prayer', sung to the tune of 'Auld Lang Syne'. An old man with his great-granddaughter muttered, 'I didn't fight in two world wars so that Cliff Richard could line his pockets by exploiting the "Lord's Prayer".'

A Scotsman behind him said, 'Aye, and the bastard's murderin' "Auld Lang Syne".'

I left the boys in the queue, and went to Boots to buy some Nurofen and a packet of Starburst (I am mildly addicted to both). As I walked through the Foxhunter Shopping Centre, I passed a fat elf smoking a cigarette. I approached the elf and said, 'Forgive me, but are you one of Santa's little helpers?' He scowled and said, 'I'm on my break. Whadja want?'

I explained about the queue in Debenhams and asked for his help, citing Glenn's Attention Deficit Disorder. On our way back to the queue, the fat elf explained that he'd just been sacked from his job as an under-manager at NatWest. He said elf work was harder than it looked – cheeriness didn't come easily to him. I sympathized.

'Perhaps we can meet up for a drink one night,' he said. I looked at his weak eyes and his beer gut spilling over his green tights, and gave him a false telephone number. The fat elf took us to the front of the queue by saying, 'Make way, make way, for this tragic family.' The queue parted with much speculation as to which of the three of us was terminally ill.

Santa was a disgrace: his beard was hanging off, and he'd made no attempt to hide his Reebook trainers. However, William was sufficiently deceived and asked for a Barbie Hairdressing Salon.

Saturday, November 27
Wisteria Walk, Ashby de la Zouch, Leicestershire

My mother married for the fourth time today. She is on the way to being the Elizabeth Taylor of Ashby de la Zouch. Unfortunately, her bridegroom, Ivan Braithwaite, had been encouraged by his night-school creative-writing teacher to write a 'millennium marriage service'. I had to look away when he turned to my mother and vowed, 'Pauline, my soon-to-be wife, I swear to love you emotionally, spiritually and physically, forever, plus one more day.'

When my mother replied, 'Ivan, my soon-to-be husband, I swear to be supportive of your life choices, aware of your hidden vulnerability, and fully cognizant of your sexual needs,' I almost ran from the registrar's office. My mother didn't actually say 'I do', because she got a rogue hat-feather stuck down her throat and had a choking fit. Does this make the marriage invalid? I hope so.

2 a.m.
Work on my serial-killer comedy for the BBC, *The White Van*. It's coming along nicely.

Wednesday, December 1
Wisteria Walk, Ashby de la Zouch, Leicestershire

I found a tin of Whopper Hot Dogs in my mother's bed this morning. It was a disturbing image; reminding me somehow of my one and only visit to Amsterdam. I was intending to wash her bed-linen as a surprise for when she returned from her honeymoon in Pompeii. But in the circumstances, I simply pulled the duvet straight and plumped up the pillows.

Thursday, December 2

After waiting three weeks, I've finally got to see the new GP, Dr Ng. I asked him if he was related to the Dr Ng in Soho, whom I occasionally consulted. He said no. I said I was surprised, as Ng was an unusual name. For some reason, he took offence at this and snapped, 'There are millions of Ngs in the world.'

I sensed that I had committed a faux pas and changed the subject to that of my health. I explained that, for some five years, I have *needed* to consume at least five packets of Opal Fruits a day. He furrowed his brow. 'Opal Fruits?' he checked.

'They've since changed the name to Starburst,' I said, unable to keep the bitterness out of my voice. I told him about the panic attack I had recently when I discovered there were no Opal Fruits in the house. Of how I had walked to the BP garage in the rain at 3 a.m. to buy some. 'Do you have any advice?' I asked.

'Yes,' he said, turning to his computer, where my records were displayed. 'Buy them wholesale.'

I had booked a double appointment, so I took my time while I filled him in about my latest phobia – falling in the crater of a live volcano. Should I seek help? 'No,' said Dr Ng, 'you should keep away from volcanoes.' For the first time in my adult life, I left the surgery without a prescription. On my way out, I asked Mrs Gringle, the receptionist, what the yellow sticker on the front of my medical records denoted. 'Time waster,' she said coldly. She has never liked our family since my mother called the doctor out on Christmas Day after my father swigged a decanter full of Stolichnaya vodka, believing it to be Malvern water.

Friday, December 3

An awkward moment at breakfast. Glenn said, 'I reckon you should tell William the truth about Father Christmas, Dad.' Apparently, William has worked out on the computer at nursery school that it would take Father Christmas 15 trillion hours to visit every child in the world. Should I continue the charade that the toys are made in Greenland by elves, or should I confess that the plastic rubbish he craves is shipped from Taiwan, then brought to Toys 'R' Us by container lorry?

Saturday, December 4

William is confused about the Blair baby. He's got it into his head, from watching the news on TV, that it will be the new Messiah. How Glenn and I laughed! Though when I asked Glenn what he knew about the Messiah, it turned out that he'd never heard of him. 'I was just laughin' to keep you company,' he said.

Sunday, December 5

Went to The Lawns for tea today with my father and his newish wife, Tania. To my joy, Pandora was there, looking ravishing in pink cashmere. I told her that I had overheard complaints in the Post Office that she was neglecting her constituents. 'I'm talking to you, aren't I?' she said, angrily. I took this opportunity to ask for her help with jumping the council house queue. She said, 'Are you mad? I couldn't possibly be seen to be helping my half-brother.' She pressed speed-dial on her mobile and left a message. 'Ken, darling! Dobbo's camp are telling the press you've caught a fatal fungal infection from the newts.' She dialled again: 'Dobbo darling, Ken's people are telling

the press you've been seen in B&Q buying a noose.'
She always was a stirrer.

Tuesday, December 7
Wisteria Walk, Ashby de la Zouch, Leicestershire

My mother returned from her honeymoon tonight.
She complained about the cold weather in Pompeii
and talked about suing Cheapo Tours. She has already
filled in one of their official complaint forms with
the lie that she was forced to buy a cashmere sweater,
pashmina shawl and a Gucci leather jacket in an
attempt to keep warm. When I pointed out to her
that it was ludicrous to have expected blue skies and
hot sun in December, she said that she was led to
believe that Vesuvius would give off 'some residual
heat'. 'By whom?' I asked. 'A geologist I met on the
net,' she replied. I advised her to drop her claim.

Wednesday, December 8

William has changed his mind about the Barbie
Hairdressing Salon. He is now demanding the same
present that Brooklyn Beckham is getting – a £45,000
toy Ferrari from Harrods.

I admit to feeling bitter and resentful about this. Beckham junior is nine months old and has never done a stroke of work in his life, yet he'll soon be driving around in the lap of luxury. Whereas I'm an involuntary pedestrian. Where is the justice in that?

Thursday, December 9

Job Centre New Deal appointment, 10.15. Catherine Root is my personal job adviser. She is personable enough, though somebody should tell her that it is possible to cure a squint these days. Ms Root wrote down my work experience and qualifications:

Librarian, civil servant with responsibility for newt and natterjack toad statistics, offal chef and TV presenter. 'Quite an eclectic mix,' I said, anxious to impress on her that I was not just any old job-seeker but had an extensive vocabulary and would be wasted sweeping leaves in the grounds of an institution.

'Do you have a degree?' she enquired, almost looking me in the eye. 'No,' I admitted, 'but I did once share a flat in Oxford with Doctor Pandora Braithwaite MP.' This was a mistake, Ms Root turned out to be a critic of Pandora's, remarking coldly that, in her opinion, she had lost touch with her constituents. When I asked for proof of this, Ms Root said Pandora had turned down a request to open the Job Centre's new toilet block, disappointing many. I left with an appointment to see a Mr Nobby Brown of Brown's Poultry at 11 a.m. tomorrow.

Friday, December 10

I am now employed as a turkey plucker. For £3.50 an hour, I pull the feathers out of recently deceased birds. I work with six women in an ill-lit shed. The noise and cackling is indescribable and the turkeys being butchered next door kick up their own hideous din, too.

11 p.m.
Went to Glenn's school tonight to see their Christmas musical, *Jesus-In-Las Vegas – A Star is Born*, written by Roger Patience the headmaster. Glenn played a croupier who helped at the birth.

Some of the audience were obviously taken aback when Mary made her entrance in a strapless sequinned evening dress, to be joined by Joseph in his tuxedo singing 'All Shook Up', but I took it in my stride. I am conversant with avant-garde theatre. I have been to the Royal Court Theatre in London several times.

Sunday, December 12

I asked Costas in the kebab shop why he was in such a bad mood tonight. 'S'that bleddy Tony Blair,' he said, hacking angrily at the doner turning on the spit. ''E broke 'is bleddy promise, init?'

'On what?' I asked. 'Onna bleddy Elgin Marbles, init?' he snarled. I mentioned to him that Turkey was about to join the EU, but not until I was leaving and was safely through the door.

Friday, December 24
Wisteria Walk, Ashby de la Zouch, Leicestershire

I thank God that my work at Brown's Poultry is seasonal and therefore over. I managed to keep my turkey-plucking job a secret from my family, though tonight my mother asked me why I had feathers in my hair. I made up the ludicrous story that a pillow had burst as I walked through Debenhams Bedding Department while Christmas shopping. She narrowed her eyes and was about to speak when Ivan called from the kitchen that the Sellotape had run out. This led to a row, with various members of the family accusing the others of wasting, hogging or using too much Sellotape while wrapping presents.

Being the only one sober, I was forced to drive to the BP garage. The shelves were empty of stationery goods, but my friend Mohammed, the manager, took pity on me and gave me some sticky-tape from the back office. It was an act of Christian charity. Later, I was blowing the feathers out of my underpants with a hairdryer when my mother barged into my room. She said, 'If you're going to indulge in bizarre sexual practices, you should put a bolt on that door.'

Christmas Day

William quickly tired of his main present, the Barbie Hair Salon: the rollers were fiddly and Barbie kept slipping out of the chair until I fastened her in with a lump of Blu-Tack. My father arrived at 11 and sneered when he saw William brushing the doll's tresses with a tiny plastic brush. 'He'll end up a bleedin' poofter,' he laughed, before thrusting an ill-wrapped present into William's arms. It was an Action Man, riding a motorbike armed with a rocket-launcher and enough ammunition to annihilate China. I said, 'I specifically requested that William was *not* to be given any gender-targeted toys.' Later, I watched in disgust as my little son made Action

Man rampage through the hair salon, kidnap Barbie and subject her to various indignities.

Boxing Day

The Moles took tea with the Braithwaites today. The atmosphere was strained to start with, and was made much worse when my mother ridiculed the Dome, saying it looked like a female porcupine about to mate. Pandora snapped that she had been invited to Millennium Eve in the Dome. I asked to see her ticket. She said it was 'in the post'.

Friday, December 31, 1999

I borrowed my mother's car and spent the evening driving Glenn and William around Leicestershire in a fruitless search for beacons and fireworks. Eventually, in Victoria Park, we came across a brazier on a pole fuelled by a cylinder of British Gas. A kindly Hindu man handed out samosas to the few spectators. When the Town Hall clock began to sound the hour, we celebrated the New Year by sharing a bottle of Morrisons Buck's Fizz with a party of drag queens dressed as Sleeping Beauty, Cinderella, Snow White, etc. William asked to be introduced to the 'beautiful princesses'. He didn't appear to notice that most of them had severe five-o'clock shadow.

When the clock struck 12 I kissed my boys, then we linked arms with strangers and attempted to sing 'Auld Lang Syne'. Some rowdy elements in the crowd sang the tune but improvised the words, bellowing scurrilous and defamatory things about Sir Cliff Richard. Later, at home, we watched as a family as the guests inside the Dome criss-crossed arms. Glenn said, 'How come the Queen don't know now to do "Auld Lang Syne" proper, Dad?' For once, I didn't correct his appalling grammar, though I have resolved to do so in the year 2000.

As I went up the stairs to bed, Ivan drunkenly whispered, 'Your mother told me about your feather fixation. Do you want to talk about it?' I resolved, at that moment, to move into 7 Scrag Close, the council house I'd previously, arrogantly, stupidly, turned down.

2000

Monday, January 3, 2000
Wisteria Walk, Ashby de la Zouch, Leicestershire

So, how do I greet the New Millennium? In despair. I'm a single parent, I live with my mother, my novels remain unpublished. My cookery book, *Offally Good*, is to be found in all bad bookshops at 59p a copy. I have a bald patch the size of a jaffa cake on the back of my head. Nobody's face lights up when I enter a room. My sons would probably miss me if I ran away, but it might take them a week or two to notice that I was gone. How did it come to this? I showed such promise when I was a youth. Why haven't *I* received my fair share of the glittering prizes? My TV celebrity in 1997 was short-lived. And, anyway, who wants to be famous for cooking offal on cable television? It's time for a total re-evaluation; I must reinvent myself. I can't go on like this, drifting into early middle age. I need a Life Plan, and one that includes my two sons.

Tuesday, January 4

This morning, I decided to involve my sons in formulating my Life Plan. I went into their bedroom and switched off the TV and removed the videotape they'd been laughing at (footage recorded from Sky News of Pandora Braithwaite and her fellow VIPs, shivering in the queue in a stiff breeze at Stratford railway station). They protested, but I said, 'We Moles must grab the New Millennium by its throat, shake it about and force it to work for us.' I gave them a pen and paper and asked them to write down their goals in life. William wrote, 'More sweets, my own telly, get a Andrex dog.' Glenn wrote, 'I should like to get married when I am 18 as I think it is a good way to get sex without going out every night. To be the runner-up to the world champion rollerblader would be quiet [sic] nice.' I challenged Glenn with this. 'Why only runner-up? Why not go all out for world champion?' I asked. 'Because I don't wanna get too famous, Dad,' he said. 'That poor little Brooklyn's 'avin' to be guarded by the SAS now, ain't 'e?' My poor son is obsessed with the gormless Beckhams and their offspring.

My own life goals are as follows: 1. Buy large detached house in respectable suburb. 2. Find soulmate with huge intellect, large earning power and substantial breasts. 3. Insist on meeting with head of BBC Drama and refuse to leave his office until he has bought *The White Van*, my comedy about a serial killer. 4. Have modest hair-weave.

Wednesday, January 5

My mother and Ivan have been in bed all day with the Australian flu. I looked in on them tonight. My mother croaked, 'About bloody time. We're dying of neglect in here.' I said, 'I was respecting your privacy.' She begged me to call out the emergency doctor, saying she felt 'desperately ill', but I refused, saying, 'We mustn't put further pressures on the National Health Service.' I mixed them each a blackcurrant Lemsip and left them to sweat it out. As I closed their bedroom door, I heard Ivan wheeze, 'I've had more compassion from the Inland Revenue.' I was woken several times in the night by their annoying coughs and feeble cries for attention. Eventually, Ivan crawled downstairs and called the doctor, who sent for an ambulance.

Thursday, January 6

My mother is now in a hospital 60 miles away, where they are treating her pneumonia. I refuse to feel guilty. Guilt is a destructive emotion and doesn't fit in with my Life Plan. I completed yet another housing form in my attempt to get a decent council house. To gain a few more points, I ticked the 'gay' box. The forms are totally confidential, so nobody outside the housing office will ever know that I am really a . . .

Friday, January 7

Too ill with flu to write much. I pray for death. Ivan found the housing application form and said to me, 'I always knew.'

Friday, January 28
Wisteria Walk, Ashby de la Zouch, Leicestershire

The Sydney Flu has swept through the Mole family like a viral hurricane and has left us traumatized and weakened. The bathroom cabinet cannot hold all the prescription drugs, so a pine shelf has been cleared of its bath oils and pressed into service. Each of us Moles developed complications. Dr Ng was at our house so often I'm surprised he didn't bring his toiletry bag and slippers. One day, after being summoned urgently to my bedside, he rang the *Lancet* on his mobile and asked if they'd be interested in a 1,000 word article on 'GP rage'.

Saturday, January 29

I received the following letter this morning.

Dear Adrian,

Remember me? I am your mother, Pauline Mole. Currently residing in bed five, ward 20, Glengorse District Hospital. I am recovering from pneumonia and pleurisy and have been here for three long weeks (on oxygen). I am very hurt that you haven't been to see me, sent me flowers or written a card. Your neglect is impeding my recovery. I can't sleep for wondering where I went wrong.

Love from your mother.

P.S. I have stopped smoking. It is too difficult to manage in an oxygen mask.

Dear Mum,

Is it really three weeks? It has gone by in a flash. I'm pleased to hear that you have stopped smoking. I have collected up the ashtrays (all 31 of them) and thrown them into the wheelie-bin so as to lessen the temptation when you get home. The reason I haven't visited you is because I am still weak from the Sydney Flu. Dr Ng was called to my bedside four times, twice in the middle of the night. You should count yourself lucky that you were given a hospital bed, even though it was 60 miles away.

I intended to send you a bouquet of flowers but, quite honestly, I was horrified at the prices they were asking. The minimum charge for a bouquet is £15! Then there is a delivery charge of £2.50. It is sheer exploitation. I concede that I could have sent you a get-well card, but a trip to the shops is out of the question until I regain the strength in my legs. Your husband, Ivan, has kept me informed about your progress. You *have* been in my thoughts and I am hurt and annoyed to be charged with neglecting you.

Your son, Adrian

I gave this note to Ivan to give to my mother. He is a fool for love, he drives 60 miles there and back a day to visit her. At 10 p.m. Ivan got back from the hospital. He was ecstatic. 'Your mother woke up this morning and asked for her make-up bag,' he said. He confided in me that when she'd first been admitted he passed her hospital bed twice without recognizing her. He'd never seen her without lipstick or mascara before. He gave me a reply from my mother.

Dear Adrian,

So, I'm not worth £17.50? When I think of the money and attention that I've lavished on you over 32 years, it makes me sick. I will probably be discharged in a couple of days. I want you gone from Wisteria Walk by then. You must take your boys and go and live with your father and Tania. There are four empty bedrooms at The Lawns.

Formally known as your mother

Sunday, January 30

Just returned from The Lawns after explaining my housing dilemma to my father and his wife, Tania. They were not exactly keen to take me and my boys in. 'We *use* those bedrooms,' said my father. 'I keep my golf clubs in one, and Tania over-winters the geraniums in another.'

'That still leaves two empty rooms,' I pointed out.

'Sadly, no,' said Tania. 'I'm in the process of turning one of those rooms into a meditation space.'

'And the last remaining room?' I enquired with a cynical sneer. My father turned away, but Tania stared me out.

'The fourth room is to be used to store my collection of Millennium Dome memorabilia,' she said. As I stumbled away from The Lawns, I dashed tears from my eyes. All hope is gone. The council estate beckons.

Monday, January 31
The Lawns, Ashby de la Zouch, Leicestershire

After a dramatic late-night phone call from my father, me and my family have been granted temporary asylum (for one week only) at the above address. Me and my boys are sharing a room with 16 over-wintering geraniums. I am sleeping on an inflatable mattress – purchased from the *Innovations* catalogue. The boys are on a double futon. I have always wondered who bought futons, now I know: it is Tania Braithwaite, my new stepmother, who loves everything Japanese. She recently re-named Henry, her Labrador puppy. He is now to be called Yoko. No wonder the creature looks confused.

It won't be long before the house has to be given a new name. The lawns have nearly all gone and have been replaced with gravel, meaningful boulders and ponds full of koi carp. 'Them fish ain't shy, Dad,' said Glenn this morning as we were passing a pond on the way to the car. 'So how come they're called *koi*?'

I was almost at his school before I realized that Glenn had made a joke. Surely this facility with puns is a sign of my eldest son's intelligence? His teachers are obviously wrong in their assessment of him. He could be the Kathy Lette of the 2000s.

I parked, as usual, on the zig-zag lines outside the infant school's entrance and was astonished to be pounced on by the headmistress, Mrs Portnoy. 'Mr Mole,' she said, 'I have repeatedly asked parents, both verbally and in writing, not to park on the zig-zag lines. Why can't you walk William to school?' I kissed William and pushed him into the playground before tackling Portnoy's complaint.

Wednesday, February 2

Am I the only one to have noticed that today's date is 2.2.2000? Nobody else has remarked on it. I rang the housing department and, after explaining my dilemma, was put through to the homeless unit. I am suspicious of anything called a *unit*. It smacks of despair and hopelessness and a dislocation from normality. I made an appointment to meet my designated housing adviser, a Ms Pigg. Why, oh why, don't these people with ludicrous names take advantage of our accessible Deed Poll laws?

Thursday, February 3

Ms Pigg is a personable young woman (breasts like large Bramley cooking apples, legs hidden under long, black skirt, first name Pamela). She was reading my application form when I entered her office. 'So,' she said, after a brief but boring exchange about the weather, 'you are a gay, single father of two boys.' I bent down to pull up my socks. I needed time to think. Should I own up to my heterosexuality or carry on with the deception – thus earning me more Housing points? Ms Pigg was looking at me sympathetically. I stroked my moustache. Ms Pigg said, 'You're obviously not comfortable with your sexuality, Mr Mole.'

I wondered what the penalty was for giving false information on an official council form. 'No,' I muttered. 'Nobody must ever find out.' Ms Pigg touched my hand. 'Trust me,' she said. The moment passed when I could have come clean. 'There's a three-bedroom house with a garden on the Gaitskell Estate . . .'

'No,' I interrupted, 'not the Gaitskell – it's populated with homophobes. Isn't there a gay-friendly enclave where people keep their houses and gardens tidy and have well-behaved pets?'

Ms Pigg frowned. 'You seem to have a very stereotypical view of gay people,' she said. 'I've just had to evict two gay men from one of our properties. They lived in total squalor and had a dog that terrorized their neighbours.'

Friday, February 4
The Lawns

Glenn has been excluded from school for spreading a rumour that the nit nurse, Mrs McKye, is a mass murderer. 'It was a joke, Dad,' he protested. 'She's been killin' nits for 30 years, five days a week.'

I explained about Harold Shipman, and advised him to keep his mouth shut about the medical profession at the moment. We move into 13 Arthur Askey Way, Gaitskell Estate, on Saturday.

Saturday, February 5
13 Arthur Askey Way, Gaitskell Estate

I cannot understand why nobody wanted to take on the tenancy of this house.

It is dry, centrally heated, has three bedrooms, a new bathroom, a well-equipped kitchen and a large through lounge. The windows are double-glazed and there is a front garden with a hard standing area for a car and a back garden with a medium-sized tree. The council has completely redecorated.

When I asked Pamela Pigg from the council's homeless unit why the house had been vacant for over a year, she said, 'I have to tell you, Mr Mole, that this house is notorious.'

She wouldn't elaborate. Perhaps a famous Leicester person lived here once. Gary Lineker, perhaps, or Willie Thorne? Both came from humble beginnings before climbing their respective ladders to the land of fame.

Glenn and William have mixed feelings about the move. They are happy to have a bedroom each, but Glenn said, 'I aint 'ard enough for the Gaitskell, Dad, and neither are you.' William asked, 'Why have all the shops got barbed wire over the windows?'

I told him a ridiculous lie about the Territorial

Army using the shopping parade for a weekend exercise, but it was obvious that even he, the most gullible of boys, didn't believe me. It has to be faced: we are living among what sociologists call 'the underclass', and what my father, reluctantly driving the box van containing my few sticks of furniture, called 'Satan's spawn'.

However, our immediate neighbours, the Ludlows, with whom we share a party wall, seem to be very quiet types. I haven't heard so much as a peep from them. I know their name because somebody has painted 'the Ludlows live here' in black gloss paint on the front of their house.

Sunday, February 6

I left the boys watching TV and walked to the newsagent's. There was a notice on the grilled door: 'Glue or cigarettes will not be served to miners, and balaclavas must be removed.' I removed my balaclava and went inside.

An Asian man stood behind the counter. A woman I took to be his wife was stocking the magazine racks with what appeared to be pornography.

'Good morning,' I said cheerfully. 'The *Observer*, please.'

'You're too late, m'duck, the vicar's been in an' got the only copy,' said the man, in a broad Leicester accent.

'You only stock one copy of a great national newspaper?' I checked.

'We got plenty more,' he said, indicating the *News Of The World*, the *People* and *Sunday Sport*.

I asked him to order two copies of the *Observer* in future. As I was leaving, I said, as pleasantly as possible, 'Isn't it against your religion to serve pornography?'

He bridled and said, 'No, I'm a Catholic, we're from Goa, an' anyway, what's wrong with the naked female body, eh? What you got against it?'

I fear I have got off on the wrong foot with the Goans. After being searched at the entrance of the mini-supermarket, Food Is U, by a fat man in a security guard's uniform, I went inside and attempted to buy some croissants and a box of fresh orange juice. I returned home with a thick-sliced loaf and a bottle of Sunny Delight. There were two aisles of cakes and biscuits, and one aisle devoted entirely to crisps and fizzy drinks.

When I have settled in, I may write to the manager and point out that he should widen his customer base.

Friday, February 11

My mother visited my new home today. She was obviously unnerved by the journey through the estate. 'You'll never survive it, Adrian,' she said. She had brought the new dog to see us, but it refused to get out of the car. I posted a Valentine to Pandora and signed it 'Oh Pandora, still adore ya'.

Sunday, February 13

The Ludlows are back from 'opening the caravan up in Chapel-Saint-Leonards'. There are two adults, six children and three big dogs. The noise is indescribable.

Monday, February 14, St Valentine's Day

Not a single card, not one.

Monday, February 28
Arthur Askey Way

Glenn returned home from school today with a letter from his physical education teacher, Mr Lunt. It said:

Dear Mr Mole,
   Glenn gave me the following note at the beginning of games today. Although it is not written in Glenn's handwriting, I feel sure that it is not written in yours either.

   I read the enclosed ill-written note. It said:

Dear Mr Lunt,
   Something tragic 'as happened to Glenn my son he has got a terminal decease and he wont live long it is only a matter of time he dous not no so dont tell him it wood be better if he did not do cross country running as it mite set him off yours sinserly Mr Mole

   Glenn broke down and admitted that he had persuaded his mother, Sharon Bott, to write the note. He said, 'I 'ate cross-country runnin', Dad. We 'ave to wear shorts an' run through villages an' the villagers laugh an' call me chicken legs.'

*

34

I confronted Sharon in her squalid kitchen, where she was defrosting chicken korma for her kids' tea. Not for the first time, I was appalled that I had once enjoyed sexual relations with this woman. She now makes Moby Dick look dainty.

As she prised the lids off the foil containers, she whined, 'I've gotta soft heart, Aidy, I don't like to think of our Glenn 'aving the piss took out of him.'

I asked her not to interfere in Glenn's education in future. She said, 'I am his mother. 'E's got 'alf my genes.'

I said, 'Yes, the grammar, punctuation and spelling genes, unfortunately.' As I was leaving, she said, 'I still love you to bits, Aidy.' I pretended not to hear her.

I wrote Mr Lunt the following reply:

Dear Mr Lunt,

My own adolescence was made a torment by taunts about my acned complexion. Glenn has a similar complex about his abnormally thin legs. Will you please allow Glenn to wear tracksuit trousers on his next cross-country run, or change the route and stick to unpopulated fields and lanes in future, thus avoiding the taunts of ignorant fox-killing, songbird-culling, hedge-removing, river-polluting country dwellers.

I remain, sir,

A. A. Mole

Tuesday, February 29

Leap Day. A letter from the Rt Hon. Neil Kinnock!
Whom I met once when I was the offal chef in Hoi
Polloi, the Soho restaurant before it was reopened as
the Oxygen Bar, H_2O.
   The letter said:

Dear Mr Mole,
   I have great pleasure in enclosing your invitation to
the Labour Party Centenary Dinner on Monday, April 10,
2000. I will be hosting the evening, and I am delighted
that once again the Prime Minister will be our guest of
honour.
   As you may expect there will be very strict security.
I regret therefore that I am unable to give you the exact
location at this stage except to say that it will be at a
central London hotel . . .

I obviously made a lasting impression on Mr Kinnock. He must have truly enjoyed his sheep's testicle
in blackcurrant coulis.

8.30 p.m.
Sharon Bott has just left this house in tears. She
arrived uninvited at 7.30 in a taxi. She produced a

bottle of Safeway's Cava, then got down on one huge knee and asked me to marry her. I turned her down. Glenn was disappointed. He said, 'I would 'ave bin the only one in our class to 'ave a mam and dad livin' together.'

Wednesday, March 1

A terse reply from Lunt:

Dear Mr Mole,
    The wearing of tracksuit trousers is prohibited during cross-country runs.
    Best wishes,
    Mr Lunt
    P. S. As a country dweller, I find your remarks about country folk extremely offensive.

Friday, March 3

My mother has just pointed to the small print at the bottom of my Centenary Dinner invitation. The tickets cost £600. I have made an optician's appointment.

Sunday, March 5

I spent the day debating with myself – should I continue to fight the tracksuit-trousers ban on Glenn's behalf or should I give in, thus subjecting the lad to mental torture during cross-country runs and possible trauma in later life? I rang around and sought the opinion of others. My father reminded me that he had 'gone out on a limb' to support me when I stood up against the tyrannical headmaster, pop-eyed Scruton, by wearing red socks to school, thereby defying the black-socks-only rule. My mother said, 'Give in, Aidy – you can't beat Jack Straw's authoritarian regime.'

I rang my MP, Pandora Braithwaite, who had joined me in my red-socks rebellion 20 years ago. She said, 'Can't talk now, darling, I've got Ken and Frank round for dinner, and I'm about to serve the pig's brains in goat's cheese.' So, it is as I suspected all along! Ken Livingstone and Frank Dobson are hand-in-glove with each other. Their true enemy is Tony Blair. They have conspired to make Mr Blair look as though he can't control his party.

After Glenn had gone to bed, I wrote to his headmaster, Roger Patience:

Dear Headmaster,

My son, Glenn Bott, has abnormally thin legs, of which he is very self-conscious. In the circumstances, would you please make an exception to your PE-shorts-only rule and allow him to wear tracksuit trousers during cross-country runs.

Yours,

A. A. Mole

Tuesday, March 7, Shrove Tuesday

Peggy Ludlow came round at tea-time to borrow flour, a lemon, eggs, milk, a frying pan and oil. I said, sarcastically, 'Wouldn't it be simpler if I made your pancakes in my kitchen?' She agreed, and the whole Ludlow family trooped round and sat in my living room watching Jerry Springer while I tossed in the kitchen until my wrist was aching.

Vince Ludlow doesn't seem to do any work, though his family are always well rigged-out in designer clothes. Peggy invades my thoughts. Today she was wearing a snakeskin sleeveless shift dress. It was the first time I'd seen her upper arms. She has several tattoos, the most recent being a depiction of Jeremy Paxman's head. When I said that I, too, was a fan of

Newsnight, she said that she had asked for Jeremy Clarkson and was suing the tattooist.

Wednesday, March 8, Ash Wednesday

My mother invited me and the boys to a No Smoking Day party to celebrate her proposed new status as a non-smoker. We arrived slightly late, at 7.30. She answered the door looking irritable: 'You've missed the ashtray-smashing ceremony.' At 7.45, she smoked her last cigarette in the garden, surrounded by family and friends. Tears ran down her tobacco-ravaged face. Ivan then ceremoniously applied a nicotine patch to her upper arm.

When I strolled back into the house, it didn't seem the same without its perpetual pall of smoke. No reply yet from Patience regarding the tracksuit trousers.

Thursday, March 9

A telephone call from the school secretary to tell me that Roger Patience can now be reached only on the following email address: patience@neilarmstrong communitycollege.com

Friday, March 10

I called on my mother unexpectedly this afternoon: she was smoking a Silk Cut, chewing Nicorette gum and had two nicotine patches on, one on each thigh. She begged me not to tell Ivan.

Saturday, March 11

I went to see Pandora at the ceremony to close down the community centre on this estate. She told me that her dinner guests were Tim Henman and Geoffrey Boycott – a grim night, then.

Sunday, March 12

The tracksuit row drags on. The headmaster is refusing to budge. I ordered Glenn to don his tracksuit before the cross-country run, and to return home if he was ordered by his PE teacher to take it off. Glenn was home by 11.15 with the following note.

Dear Mr Mole,
    As I have stated ad nauseam, Glenn is not allowed to

wear a tracksuit during cross-country runs. It was the wearing of shorts and vests in sub-zero temperatures that put the backbone into our young men and enabled our great country to win two world wars and a fistful of rowing medals at the Atlanta Olympics in 1996.

Yours,

R. Patience (Chief Executive)

Neil Armstrong Community College

I rang Pandora at the Commons and was put through to a call centre where a recorded voice told me to press the star button if I was a constituent, or the hash button if I had a complaint about the NHS, street lighting or council house transfers.

I listened in fury as the voice took me through numbers one to eight before telling me to 'press button nine if you wish to speak to a person directly'. 'At last,' I said, 'I get to speak to Pandora.' But it wasn't she. It was Lorraine from the call centre, who, after an acrimonious exchange, informed me that 'my call was being recorded'.

I rang my new stepmother (and Pandora's mother), Tania, and asked for Pandora's email address. 'I'm cleaning out the koi carp pond, Adrian,' she said. 'Could you ring me back at a more convenient time?'

'So, you are putting your koi carp pets in front of your step-grandson's dilemma, are you?' I said angrily.

'As a matter of fact, I am,' she snapped. 'I agree with Patience. Shorts and vests did make this country great.' It's true: advancing age does turn people right-wing. Tania used to be a leading radical in the political circles of Ashby de la Zouch.

Tuesday, March 14

Now William is in trouble at school for opining that Posh Spice should be the next Queen of England. According to him, Mrs Claricoates, his teacher, made him sit in the Wendy-and-Kevin house alone during storytime. As a punishment, I know that's not exactly in the bamboo-under-the-fingernails league, but he was still upset when he got home and totally confused about the hereditary principle.

I kept Glenn at home today while I considered my next move in the tracksuit row: a letter to the awkward squad, MP Jeremy Corbyn? Alert the *Leicester Mercury*? Or a petition?

Wednesday, March 15

Vince Ludlow has been arrested for failing to pay £140 arrears! Four policemen served a warrant on him at 7.30 a.m. Apparently, he was fined £280 in October 1997. He stole the brass knob from the door of the magistrate's court after celebrating his birthday at Snobs in town. Peggy was distraught as, from our respective doorsteps, we watched the police van turn the corner. She sobbed, 'Vince gone, and not a bleedin' fag in the 'ouse.'

Thursday, March 16

My father is worried about Longbridge. 'It's bloody tragic. How'm I gonna get spares for the Rover?'

Saw Lizzie Broadway, my old schoolfriend, in the newsagent's. She was buying cat food. I asked if she lived on the estate. 'God, no,' she said. 'Do I look socially excluded?' before hurrying towards her BMW on the kerb, where a gang of local lads were measuring the hub caps with a tape measure.

Friday, March 17, St Patrick's Day

Pandora rang and ordered me to stop harassing her. In only three minutes she used the words 'clear' or 'clearly' 19 times. Is it now compulsory for politicians to use this word?

Monday, March 20

Glenn's photograph is on the front of tonight's *Ashby Bugle*. The headline said, 'GLEN CROSS ABOUT COUNTRY RUN'. It was not a flattering portrait: the combination of his new Beckham haircut and the way he was scowling into the sun gave him the brutal look of a youth at a fascist training camp. As I paid for my copy, a pensioner behind me looked at Glenn and said, 'I wunt like to meet him on pensions day.'

I longed to tell the mustachioed lard-belly that Glenn was a good boy, but she picked an argument with the newsagent about non-delivery of her *People's Friend*, so I left without defending my son. When I got home, I read the article with growing disgust; it was littered with inaccuracies.

To the Editor, the Ashby Bugle
Dear Sir,

It is not my habit to write to the papers, but I must on this occasion as you have written an ill-informed and inaccurate article about my son, Glenn, and his refusal to wear shorts during cross-country running at his school, Neil Armstrong Comprehensive.

1) Glen is Glenn. You misspelt his name throughout.
2) I am Adrian Mole, not A. Drain-Mole.

3) I am 33 years old, not 73.
4) I am not 'unemployed'; I am currently writing a serial-killer-comedy for the BBC called *The White Van*.
5) Glenn does not wear an earring in his right ear. He wears it in his left lobe.
6) Glenn does not have the support of our MP, Dr Pandora Braithwaite. She refused to back our campaign. I quote from her recent email: 'I am too fg busy with the Onion Working Party to faff about with fg school uniform issues.'

I remain, sir, yours,

A. Mole, father of Glenn

Tuesday, March 21

Glenn came to me tonight as I was ironing and listening to *The Archers*. He begged me to allow him back to school, and said he would happily wear white shorts on cross-country runs. I reminded him that *Midlands Today* was interested in covering his campaign on its news spot.

He said, 'It's not my campaign any more, Dad. It's yours.' As I ironed his white shorts, I reflected on the sacrifices parents make for their children. I'll be a laughing stock at the next parents' evening.

Thursday, March 23

The following letter was in the *Bugle* tonight.

Dear Editor
    The BBC would like to make it clear that Adrian Mole has not been commissioned by us to write a serial-killer-comedy called *The White Van*.
    Yours sincerely,
    Geoffrey Perkins (Head of Comedy)

So, the BBC now employs spies to read the regional newspapers, does it? Institutional paranoia or what?

Friday, March 24

Pamela Pigg from the homeless unit called round on her way home from work, to tell me there's a vacant maisonette on the Prescott Estate. 'It's a new housing complex, purpose-built for tenants aspiring to join the new middle class.'
    She said that Alan Titchmarsh had been consulted about the design of the patio/wheelie-bin area. He had declined, but, as Pamela said, 'At least he was consulted.'

I made her a cup of Kenco and broached the delicate matter of changing her name by Deed Poll. She got very defensive and said there had been a Pigg in the Domesday Book, a Pigg at Ypres and recently a Pigg had been awarded an OBE for services to the post office. When I said tentatively, 'Yes, but how can a Mole go out with a Pigg?' she said shyly, 'Well, we'd be Pamela and Adrian, wouldn't we?'

Saturday, March 25

Pamela and I had our first tryst watching the boat race. I bet her £500 that Cambridge would win, but I don't care. I think I may be in love with a woman called Pigg.

Tuesday, March 28

It's Pamela! Pamela! Pamela! I keep whispering her name to myself. However, I don't whisper her surname – Pigg – though I remain optimistic that she will eventually seize the day and change her name by Deed Poll.

But oh, those sublime three syllables: Pam-e-la. It's Abba's music! It's a mountain stream. It's Leicester

Town Hall gardens with the cherry blossom out. It's Edward Heath's laugh. It's a refrigerated Crunchie bar.

But Pigg. Pigg is brutish and short. It's slurry. It's the Queen Mother's teeth. It's that local authority prickly stuff that thrives next to inner ring roads. It's the predictable twist at the end of a Jeffrey Archer story. It's Ann Widdecombe's fringe.

Wednesday, March 29

Am I in love? I rang my best friend Nigel at work, and he faxed me a questionnaire. Some of the questions were relevant, some were not. He told me that if I answer yes to any four, then I am definitely in love. He had scribbled on the bottom that the questionnaire was obviously prepared for gay men, but it probably works for straights, too.

a) Do you think about him constantly?
b) Have you had your chest hair waxed?
c) Do you ring him more than four times a day?
d) Have you stopped going to saunas?
e) Are you afraid to have your hair cut in case he doesn't like it?
f) Are you writing overwrought poetry about nature?

I sat at the kitchen table with a cup of Kenco and a ballpoint, and quickly found out that I am in love with Pamela Pigg. I rang her at the housing office to tell her so (my fifth call of the day), but the senior housing officer, Terry Nutting, told me that he had given Pamela 'compassionate leave' to have her hair done.

Nutting thinks he is such a wit. He'll be laughing on the other side of his beardy face when Pamela leaves to become my wife. According to Pammy, Nutting is an incompetent idler who sits all day in his office answering the personal ads in *Private Eye*.

She said, in that sweet voice of hers (like a zephyr blowing across a linnet's egg), 'Terry Nutting wouldn't recognize a homeless person if he fell over one in a shop doorway.'

Friday, March 31

Pamela's new hairstyle is growing on me. Not, of course, literally growing on me. What I mean is that I can now glance in her direction for seconds at a time without flinching. I still think it was a mistake to go quite so short: her head is a rather peculiar shape, and her scalp is criss-crossed with scars and the evidence of childhood accidents.

Saturday, April 1, April Fool's Day

At 11.30 a.m., my sister Rosie rang to say that there was a letter at their house addressed to me from Greg Dyke, head bloke at the BBC, to say that he had read *The Restless Tadpole*, my epic poem, and wanted Andrew Davies to adapt it for BBC2. When I asked her to fax me the letter, she laughed her horrible laugh and put the phone down.

Sunday, April 2

So, I have reached the age of 33 – the same age as Jesus was when he was killed. Glenn gave me a card which said on the front in gothic print 'Happy Birthday Single Father'. There was a picture of a man with a moustache standing on a hump-backed bridge and staring down into a river – as though he was thinking about throwing himself in. Perhaps to escape his responsibilities. William had made a card at nursery school out of egg shells, lentils and crushed cornflakes. I thanked him but privately thought it was disgusting, especially when half the world is starving.

Monday, April 3

My love affair with Pamela moved into a sexual stage tonight, though 'full union', as she calls it, has yet to take place. Pamela is a fan of the female condom, but, after examining one she took out of her briefcase, we discovered that it had been issued in 1998. We decided not to risk it. Pam was keen to consummate, saying, 'I just want to get it out of the way, Adrian.'

I explained that I hadn't kept condoms in the house since William took one to nursery school as his contribution to the hot-air-balloon mural. It was an eagle-eyed Ofsted inspector who spotted the 'big boy arouser' rising between the cotton-wool clouds.

Pamela asked me if I'd like to go to Stockport next weekend to meet her parents. I lied and said, 'Yes, Wiggly.' She asked me to call her Wiggly. She calls me Snuffly. I've had a slight head cold since we met.

Tuesday, April 4

The Ludlows held a welcome home from prison party for Vince tonight. I went next door at 10 p.m., after William and Glenn had gone to bed. I don't want my boys to associate the word 'prison' with the word 'party'. Vince said he had seen Jonathan Aitken in the prison chapel, and had witnessed Mr Aitken's religious fervour. Vince said, ''E was shakin' 'is tambourine so 'ard that 'is Rolex fell off.' Vince told me to back Papillon in the Grand National. I said it was highly unlikely that another son/jockey and father/trainer combination would win.

I rang Pamela as soon as I got home. She said she was in bed with a Trollope. 'Anthony or Joanna?' I asked. Pamela laughed, as though I'd made a joke.

Thursday, April 6

The Piggs don't like children, so my mother is babysitting William for the weekend and Glenn is going to his mother's.

Pamela warned me tonight not to tell her father that I am an unpublished poet and novelist. I pointed out that I have published two cookery books: *Offaly Good* and *Offaly Good Again*. She told me that her father was a militant vegetarian and a former RAF kayak instructor. I dread meeting Mr Pigg.

Friday, April 7
The Olde Forge, Stockport

He is even worse than I feared. 'Call me Porky!' he boomed. He was wearing a sort of fleecy Babygro garment and rubber socks. He had just returned from a training session on an artificial slalom course on the River Tees. He has offered to take me down the rapids in his double kayak on Sunday. Mrs Pigg was loading her van in preparation for a country fayre, at which she sells the hedgehog boot scrapers she makes out of pine cones and plastic bristles.

As Mrs Pigg was showing me to my single bed, she asked me to call her Snouty. When I enquired what her real Christian name was, she glared and said, 'Why are you presuming that my parents were Christians?' I told her I'd seen the photograph on the mantelpiece of her parents' wedding, which had been taken outside a church and been attended by a vicar holding a copy of the Old Testament. She said that I 'mustn't bother' Pamela in the night, as Mr Pigg did not approve of sex before long-term commitment.

Saturday, April 8

The Piggs took me to a Beefeater restaurant for dinner tonight. A cardboard cut-out of the TV chef Brian Turner welcomed us in. The conversation ground to a halt over pre-dinner drinks, when Porky discovered that I am a single father living in a council house. The tension was palpable. Pamela developed a most unflattering tic in her left eye.

But all was not lost, because Porky and I chose the lightly breaded deep-fried mushrooms at £2.95 (with a choice of two dips). Porky and I now have something in common: we will talk about our Beefeater experience for many years to come.

Thank you, Mr Turner.

Monday, April 10

William woke up screaming in the night. He'd been having a nightmare about his forthcoming SAT exams. He was mostly incoherent, but I managed to glean that his nightmare included David Blunkett's guide dog and the gay Teletubby, Tinky Winky. I didn't press him for details.

Pamela hasn't rung me since our weekend with her

parents. I fear that beside the hirsute masculinity of her father I appear a poor specimen. My expert knowledge of the early poetry of Philip Larkin cannot compete with Porky Pigg's ability to roll a double kayak in white water. I could tell that my refusal to join Porky in his flimsy plastic boat sowed doubts in Pamela's mind.

Did some primeval instinct warn her that my spermatozoa and her eggs were incompatible and wouldn't add to the quality of the gene pool? Am I doomed to have yet another failed relationship? Whatever – as they say on *Jerry Springer* – she was very quiet as we drove south and didn't offer her tongue when I kissed her goodnight.

Tuesday, April 11

This morning, I handed William his usual carrier bag full of toilet rolls and squashed cereal packets and was amazed when he handed it straight back to me, saying, 'We can't play at school any more, Dad, so don't collect 'em up.'

At home time, I broke the rules and waited outside William's classroom. On looking through the glass panel in the door I saw that the children were sitting in rows being taught exam techniques by an 'exam trainer'. (Formerly known as a teaching assistant.) The weather chart and the nature table were nowhere to be seen. The hamster cage was empty. There were various exhortations around the room. As I watched, the exam trainer wrote 'Exams are good, play is bad' on the white board. The children dipped their pens in their inkwells and copied this slogan down. Since when has it been compulsory to write in ink? I fear that once again Mrs Parvez, the headmistress, has misinterpreted education-department guidelines. She won't be content until the children are wearing wooden clogs.

Wednesday, April 12

I embarked on a new novel, *Sty*, today. Progress was slow. I only managed to write 104 words, including the title and my name.

Sty, by Adrian Mole.

The pig grunted in its sty. It was deeply sad. Somehow it felt different from the other pigs with which it shared a home. 'Look at them,' thought the pig. 'They are oblivious to the fact that they are merely part of the food chain.' The pig had felt discontented since it had glimpsed Alain de Botton's TV programme, *Philosophy: A Guide To Life*, through a gap in the pig farmer's curtain. The wisdom of Socrates, Epicurus and Montaigne had brought home to the pig that it was completely uneducated and knew nothing of the world beyond the sty.

He glanced over at the sty to where Pamela Pigg was grunting with pleasure as she stuck her hairy, wet snout into the trough. He had been in love with Pamela for years but now he wondered if she was his intellectual equal. There was something about her piggy eyes that repelled him . . .

NOTES ON NEW NOVEL: 1. Should the pig have a name? 2. Should the pig's thoughts be in quotes? 3. Has the story got legs? Or is the main protagonist (the pig) too restricting a character, i.e., being (a) unable to communicate with the other pigs and (b) never leaving the sty?

Sunday, April 16

Pamela Pigg has just left this house after flying into a rage and accusing me of stealing her life and turning it into 'fifth-rate art'. She read my manuscript of *Sty* which I had foolishly left on the kitchen table under a copy of *Men's Health*. As she ran to her car, I shouted, 'I'm an artist. We must forage where we can for our materials.'

Pamela shouted back, 'I'm a housing officer. We must cancel the artist's move to a maisonette as promised.' I went inside and read page 124 of *Men's Health* – bed-busting sex – for my art, of course.

Monday, April 17
Arthur Askey Way

William begged me for £2.49 today. He wants to buy a booster pack of Pokémon cards. When I refused, he burst into tears and threw himself down on the kitchen floor. Glenn came in and said, 'You've gotta give 'im the money, Dad, he's lost respect in the playground.'

Apparently, there are 151 characters in a set and William has only collected 37 of the most common. Glenn said, 'It's like, you know, wearing Marks & Spencer's trainers, Dad?' Glenn has never forgiven me. I once made him go to school in my old Marks & Spencer trainers when his own Nikes had disappeared. He still wakes in the night sweating and crying out for Childline.

Tuesday, April 18

Tania rang at 10.30 this morning to tell me that my father had fallen off a ladder while trying to construct a pagoda in their garden and had injured his back. He was waiting for an ambulance, she said. I could hear my father groaning in the background and the sound of splashing and birdsong.

I left William and Glenn next door with the Ludlows and hurried off to The Lawns. My father was lying half in, half out of the koi carp pool and appeared to be in agony. Tania was squatting by his side, instructing him to 'breathe the pain away, George'. The ambulance took another hour to arrive, having been misdirected by the computer to The Mental Health Unit in Rutland. The ambulance-men, Derek and Craig, were remorselessly cheerful. It was their fifth gardening incident in two days. They blamed Alan Titchmarsh for the recent alarming rise in accident and emergency admissions. Tania stayed behind to calm the carp and pack a bag, and I went in the ambulance with my father. To take his mind off his pain, I tried to engage him in conversation about Charlie Dimmock, but he wasn't interested.

At 2 o'clock in the afternoon he was diagnosed as

having two cracked vertebrae, a fractured shoulder and a deep cut in his left thigh caused by the Homebase Spend & Save card in his trouser pocket. At 8.30 p.m. he was finally taken up to Bevan Ward and put into a bed. Without his teeth, and with his grey hair sticking up around his head, he looked every one of his 56 years. He is lying flat on his back and is unable to do the slightest thing to help himself. 'So, not much change there, then,' said my mother, his ex-wife, when I rang to give her a progress report.

Query: Where can I buy two Pokémon Easter eggs?

Wednesday, April 19

When I visited my father today, I found him in considerable distress. The hospital has lost his teeth. 'Not that it bloody well matters,' he gummed, 'I couldn't reach my bleedin' food anyway.' Apparently, his breakfast tray had been placed 6 in. out of reach of his good arm, 2 in. nearer than the emergency call button. He is worried about Tania's reaction when she sees him for the first time without his teeth. Apparently, she is under the impression that his teeth are his own.

*

Pamela Pigg rang to tell me that she wants to renew our relationship. She has bought the boys two Pokémon Easter eggs. I said yes.

Sunday, April 23, Easter Day, St George's Day, Shakespeare's birthday

I didn't know which trousers to put on today, or what to have for breakfast. Am I suffering from the modern illness, Choice Overload Syndrome? I just can't decide. Somebody has written N F R O T H in red pen on my father's notes. I asked a junior doctor what it stood for. 'Not for resuscitation, over the hill,' she said, and hurried away. I hope this was a joke. When I wished Pamela a happy St George's Day this morning, she accused me of 'celebrating fascism'. We are doomed. Doomed.

Tuesday, April 25

My father begged me to help him escape from the hospital this afternoon. He said he is losing the will to live due to lack of sleep and the pain from his bed sores. His false teeth have not turned up, despite a top-level internal inquiry. He is living on soup and porridge – when somebody remembers to feed him. He is almost entirely helpless.

Personally, I blame Tania, his new wife, for his accident. My father is too old to be up a ladder trying to construct a Japanese-style pagoda under her exacting instructions. I have suggested to the rest of the family that we arrange a rota so that one of us is always in attendance at hospital meal times.

I rang Pandora at her Westminster office and asked her to visit the hospital incognito. I said that she should see the third-world conditions for herself. She said she would 'drop in if she could', but she was 'terribly busy' with Frank Dobson's mayoral election. I laughed a hollow laugh and said did she realize it was Anzac Day, the anniversary of a similarly doomed campaign.

Thursday, April 27
Bevan Ward

A letter from Nigeria written by my ex-wife, Jo-Jo, mother of William and heiress of a lorry tyre manu-facturer's fortune. I live in dread of Jo-Jo sending for William when Nigeria's Civil War is over.

Dear Adrian,

Your mother has written to tell me that William is living in 'morally dubious circumstances'. She writes that he mixes with criminals 'on a daily basis'. Can this be true? I have looked at Arthur Askey Way using the world wide web satellite and was disturbed to see a burned-out car in front of your house. I also saw that your front garden was extremely squalid. Is that the mattress we used to sleep on?

Please do not forget, Adrian, that William is part Nigerian and is the grandson of a chief. It is essential that he is brought up extremely carefully. My circumstances are such that I cannot send for him at present, so I beg you to move William away from the Gaitskell Estate before his character and personality are irrevocably damaged.

I have tried to reach you on the telephone, but a recorded voice tells me 'it has not been possible to connect your call'. I looked you up on the net and was alarmed to see that you are considered a bad credit risk and that you owe £75.31 to your newsagent, £43.89 to your milkman and to BT £254.08. A further search revealed that you are overdrawn at the bank by £947.16. I scrolled on further and found that you withdrew all monies from your savings account with the Market Harborough Building Society on December 19, 1999. This money was put aside to pay for William's piano lessons. Is he having them?

I am very concerned about your mental health. A search of your medical records revealed to me that you visited your doctor's surgery three times last month, complaining that you were being spied upon. Your doctor has written on your notes 'could be mildly paranoiac'. Please contact me at jojomole@aol.com

So, 1984 is here in the year 2000. It is the end of privacy. I may as well walk naked through the streets shouting out the small details of my life.

I went to see my mother and charged her with gross disloyalty. She was unrepentant. She said, 'William spends too much time playing round at the Ludlows' house.' She said, 'Vince Ludlow is a career criminal, for Christ's sake!' I have to admit, Diary, that William's frame of reference has widened lately. Last night I overheard him saying to Glenn, 'Mad Frankie Fraser was well harder than Charlie Kray.'

Saturday, April 29

I asked Pamela Pigg about that maisonette she promised me. She said (with relish, I thought), 'I've let it to a family of asylum seekers.' I asked her to arrange a swap. She said, 'They're not that desperate.'

Monday, May 1
Arthur Askey Way

I was driving my mother to the hospital today to visit her ex-husband and my father (the same man). We were sharing a jumbo-sized Mars bar in a companionable sort of way – taking alternate bites – when I was pulled over by a police car.

I was not drunk or drugged, and I had been keeping to the speed limit. I asked my mother if she had made a rude gesture to them via the rear-view mirror. She denied it. I was, therefore, baffled as to why I'd been stopped. Two policemen got out of the car. Policeman One said: 'Would you step out of your vehicle please, sir.' I did as he asked. Policeman Two said: 'You like a bit of chocolate, do you, sir?' in a sneering kind of way.

'I am a bit of a chocoholic, actually,' I joked.

'Like to munch on the cocoa solids in your vehicle, do you, sir?' said Number One.

I was slightly baffled, but answered, 'Yes, I usually buy some chocolate when I fill up with petrol.'

My mother had been listening to our conversation with ill-concealed irritation. 'It's not against the law to eat in your own car, is it?' she snapped.

Policeman Number One slowly walked round

to the front passenger window. My mother wound it down. 'It is against the law to drive without due care and attention, madam,' he said. 'And that jumbo Mars bar was being passed between you and the driver of the car like a parcel at a kiddies' tea party.'

'The policemen in *The Bill* are always driving and stuffing their faces,' she said.

I saw a nerve twitch just above his temple, and he ordered my mother out of the car while he and his colleague examined the interior. (Looking for what: Twix, Smarties, Aeros?)

We were late getting to the hospital. My father's catheter had become detached. While we waited for two clean sheets to be found from somewhere in the hospital, I watched Beryl, the privatized cleaner, push a filthy, ragged mop around the ward floor. I shuddered to think of the viruses swarming on the end of that mop. I hoped that they hadn't encamped into my father's bed sores.

Wednesday, May 3

What has happened to *The Archers*? It was once possible to listen to it in the company of the young and impressionable. Now, I have to switch off if Glenn or William are in the kitchen.

The love scenes between Sid Perks and Jolene are audible pornography. It is like overhearing two wart-hogs mating. Will somebody please put Cathy Perks in the picture? And will the person in charge of accents at the BBC teach that sexual-harassment bloke, Simon, how to speak Canadian?

Judging by the present storyline, I predict that a socially concerned villager will soon suggest that Ambridge needs a youth club. Suggested script:

JILL ARCHER: (with warm concern): Have you seen the graffiti on Uncle Tom's gravestone, 'Sid Perks is tooling Jolene'?

SOCIALLY CONCERNED VILLAGER (with liberal concern): Yes, and I deplore the damage done to the statue of Walter Gabriel on the village green.

JILL ARCHER: Yes, it was cruel to stuff an organic turnip up his . . .

SOCIALLY CONCERNED VILLAGER (interrupting): It's the set-aside generation, Jill. They've nowhere to go and nothing to do. What they need is a youth club.

JILL ARCHER: Do you think so? Do you really think so?

Dum De Dum De Dum De Dum Dum De Dum De Dum Dum, etc.

Friday, May 5

Pandora is busy absolving herself from any blame for Mr Dobson's abysmal result in the mayoral election. She said, 'I begged him to shave off that bloody beard, lose weight, buy a new suit, dye his hair, get his teeth straightened and whitened. He's only got himself to blame.'

Saturday, May 6
Ashby de la Zouch

My mother rang me this morning and asked if I would give her driving lessons. I laughed for quite a long time. Eventually, she said, 'Yes or no?' I said, 'It would be disastrous, you can't even tell left from right.' I asked her if she had requested that her new husband teach her. She said, 'Ivan reckons that there are enough cars on the road already.' I advised her to use public transport. She said that there was no public transport to the crème de la crème of boot fairs at Saddington in the middle of the Leicestershire countryside.

'Why won't Ivan take you to Saddington?' I asked.

'Ivan is a chartered accountant – he gets nervous

seeing so many cash transactions taking place between untrained amateurs,' she said.

Ivan used to be the chief accountant at the Co-op dairy until the cold winds of change knocked the milk bottles off the steps of time and replaced them with the cardboard carton in the supermarket chill cabinet.

My mother was still blathering on: 'The last time we went to a boot fair, Ivan completely ruined my pleasure by moaning about the lack of regulations. He said that both the buyers and the sellers were anarchists, and should be made to pay tax and VAT. He has even asked Pandora to bring in an act of parliament: The Boot Fair Regulation Act.'

When she mentioned that there were Abba LPs and memorabilia for sale, I offered to take her one Sunday.

Monday, May 8

My father continues to deteriorate in hospital. He has now contracted a virus (the one caused by privatized cleaning) and is in an isolation ward. Tania is in almost permanent attendance. She is taking advantage of his weakened state to read Great Literature at him. She is currently halfway through *Moby Dick*. When she went out to go to the toilet, I asked my father how he was enjoying Melville's extraordinary allegorical seafaring tale. 'I am not enjoying it,' he whined. 'I don't like fishing.'

I noticed that Tania had placed a copy of *Silas Marner: The Weaver Of Raveloe* on the bedside trolley. It was obviously to be the next literary read-aloud treat. I wondered if I should mention to her that my father has a violent antipathy to books, films and TV dramas about children. (Something had once happened to him in a cinema during the showing of a Shirley Temple film – I don't know what, but a gabardine mac was involved.)

Tania would be on firmer ground if she stuck to Raymond Chandler or the earlier Dick Francis.

Friday, May 12

Pamela Pigg called round to say that she's found me a small town house overlooking a canal basin in Leicester. The present occupant, a Mrs Wormington, is an OAP. She is in hospital, but chose to be nil by mouth, so Pamela reckons I can probably move in in a couple of weeks. I said, 'Is she nil by mouth so as to free up the country's housing stock?'

Pamela said, 'She is occupying a three-bedroom house and she is 97 years old.'

I said, 'Pamela, I don't want Mrs Wormington killed so that I can enjoy watching the narrowboats pass by my living-room window.' I asked which hospital Mrs Wormington was in. She told me that it was the same one as my father, Pankhurst Ward – which was sort of appropriate. Though Mrs Pankhurst chose to be nil by mouth.

Sunday, May 14

Mrs Wormington is nil by mouth because she has had a stroke and can't swallow properly. She has no family or friends: 'They've all died off, lad,' she told me. I used a cotton bud dipped in water to moisten her mouth. 'I don't like to bother the nurses,' she croaked.

Are pensioners to be my albatross? I can already feel her liver-spotted hand round my neck.

Wednesday, May 17

After a visit to my father, who has been urged by Tania to sue the hospital for neglect and loss of dentures, I went to Pankhurst Ward to see Mrs

Wormington. She is still nil by mouth, though there is now some doubt as to her swallowing ability.

I was there when a young doctor, in jeans and T-shirt (slogan: 'Trust me, I'm a journalist'), bellowed, 'We've asked Mrs Namole, the ear, nose and throat consultant, to have a look at you, Mrs Wormington.' I asked if this meant that Mrs Wormington could drink a cup of tea. 'Not yet. We don't want to risk her choking to death,' she said. 'I shall die if I don't have a cup of tea soon,' rasped Mrs Wormington. The doctor hurried off down the ward. I followed her. 'When will the consultant next be on the ward?' I said. 'Mrs Namole's next ward round is on Friday afternoon,' she said.

When the tea trolley came round, I placed myself between it and Mrs Wormington, but she heard the wheels. 'I've drank eight cups of tea a day for 90-odd years,' she choked. The poor woman ought by right to be admitted to the Priory. She is doing the equivalent of coming off crack.

When I went into the sluice room to find a vase for the carnations I'd bought, I heard a registrar at the nurses' station whining about the 'bed-blockers'. When I said goodbye to Mrs Wormington, she said, 'Tara lad, God bless, see you tomorrow.' I'm trapped! Trapped!

Another pensioner has broken into my life and is holding me to ransom.

Friday, May 19

Glenn asked why the washing line was full of winceyette nighties and big knickers. I explained about Mrs Wormington and he said, 'I'm relieved, Dad, I thought you was on the turn.'

Saturday, May 20

I woke with a jolt at 3 a.m. just as Leo Blair was being born (am I psychically connected to Cherie?). I went downstairs to discover that Pamela Pigg had shoved a note through the letterbox at some time during the night. On pink Filofax paper, she had written:

Dear Adrian,
   I went out on a hen night with the girls from the homeless unit tonight. Phillipa, the one with the teeth, is getting 'married' to Mary, the one with the nose, on Wednesday morning. We went to Humperdink's, the new nightclub in Melton Mowbray. I felt terribly out of place. It was full of teenage girls wearing very small

garments. I felt horribly frumpy in my Principles polka-dot outfit. It's the last time I follow the advice of the *Leicester Mercury*'s fashion correspondent.

However, the point is, Adrian, the DJ played our song, 'My Heart Will Go On'. I had to leave the dance floor. Do you remember your emotional state when we came out of the multiplex, after seeing the Leonardo Di Caprio fanclub's special showing of *Titanic*? It was the first time I had seen a grown man cry. I felt very privileged. I miss you, Adrian. Can we try again? It was stupid of me to have flown into a temper over your silly pig book.

Love, forever,

Pammy

P.S. Mary and Phillipa say you are welcome to come to the wedding. I am to be their best person. No presents, but donations to the Fawcett Society appreciated.
P.P.S. I've had disturbing thoughts of yielding myself to you.

Talk about blackmail! If I attend the lesbian wedding with her, she will 'yield' to me, will she? As if I would spend another minute in the company of a woman who flew into a feminist rage when she discovered a copy of Philip Larkin's *Diaries* on my bookshelf.

Wednesday, May 24

The wedding went off all right. I was the only man there. Even the registrar was a woman. Is this the beginning of the end for men? Pamela came back to Arthur Askey Way, but refused to 'yield' to me when she saw Kingsley Amis's *Letters* on my bedside table and Mrs Wormington's knickers on the line.

Sunday, May 28
Ashby de la Zouch

The resemblance between Leo Blair and William Hague is uncanny. Each is the other's doppelganger. Put Mr Hague in a romper suit, bootees and a woolly hat, and he is the living embodiment of Master Blair. Can Cherie and William account for their movements on the day of Leo's conception? I wouldn't be surprised if, even as I write, Mr Blair is angrily confronting a tearful Mrs Blair at Chequers. And Ffion must have seen Leo's photograph and questioned her husband's fidelity.

My mother shares my suspicions – we have several children in our family whose paternity remains a mystery. If I were Mr Blair, I would demand a DNA test immediately. How can he concentrate on affairs of state or face Mr Hague across the dispatch box until he knows the Truth?

Incidentally, if my long-held theory is true (that William Hague is Margaret Thatcher's love child) this would mean that young Leo has Thatcher's blood in his veins. I do not usually prescribe to conspiracy theories, but in this case I feel compelled to warn somebody – but who?

Tuesday, May 30

Pandora is in the constituency tomorrow. She is the guest of honour at the closing-down ceremony at St Barnabas' Library. The barbecue in the library car park starts at 6.30 p.m. I may take the boys. I will also voice my fears to Pandora about the right-wing blood alliance of Blair, Hague and Thatcher.

Wednesday, May 31

It was a painful sight to see hardbacks being used to fuel the cooking of WhoppaBurgers and Buy A Big Boy Hot Dog. The newly retired librarian, Mrs Froggatt, threw a few Barbara Cartlands on to the barbecue when the heat died down. They flared up with an eerie, pink glow. I managed to save some P. G. Wodehouses and William Browns from the flames, but there was nothing I could do for the others. Glenn couldn't watch. 'It ain't right, Dad,' he said. Underneath his rough exterior, he is quite a sensitive lad.

Pandora turned up at 7 p.m. and made a speech saying that libraries are now redundant due to the growth of the internet. One old man in the crowd shouted: 'I can't afford to go on-line on 75p a week!'

I tried to talk to Pandora about my suspicions regarding Leo Blair, but she was in a hurry to get away, having realized that being photographed in front of a pyre of books was a potential public-relations disaster.

Thursday, June 1

Mrs Wormington is well enough to come out of hospital. Her son, Ted, turned up out of the blue and tried to persuade her to go into a nursing home. I was visiting her at the time with Glenn and William. She hadn't seen Ted for 21 years, because of a row about a clock. She was adamant that she wanted to return to her own home. Ted said: 'You're being daft,

Mam. You can't live on your own at the age of 97. If you won't go into a nursing home, you'll have to come and live with me and Eunice.' A look of horror passed over her multi-wrinkled face. While Ted went to telephone Eunice, Mrs Wormington clutched at my sleeve. She said, 'Don't let him take me to live with him and Eunice. I'll be dead in a week. That Eunice is a miserable bugger – she's never been known to crack her face.' When Ted came back, he said that Eunice was still resentful about the clock. Glenn announced, 'It's all right, she's comin' 'ome with us.' I could easily have killed him.

Friday, June 2

Mrs Wormington has been slagging off the Queen Mother. 'She's never done a hand's turn in her life,' she said. 'No wonder she's always smilin'.' She moves in with us tomorrow. The adult Pampers delivery service has been alerted.

Saturday, June 3
Ashby de la Zouch

Because of Mrs Wormington's advanced age, it is like having a living history book permanently open on the kitchen table. A mention of Dunkirk brings an anecdote about her younger brother Cedric on his little boat, the *Betty Grable*, that sailed across the English Channel during the evacuation. 'He weren't the same when he came back,' she said. 'He took up knitting and joined the Communist Party.' Apparently, both of these activities were enough to banish him from the bosom of the Wormington family. 'I used to write to him in secret,' she said. 'And on his birthday I'd send him a knitting pattern.' William and Glenn have been glued to the Dunkirk coverage across television, hoping to see Cedric on the *Betty Grable*.

Sunday, June 4

My mother came round to stay with Mrs Wormington and the boys while I went to see my father in hospital. His original injuries are healing, but he is still ill with the infection he caught in hospital.

Apparently, his body has shrugged off most of the powerful antibiotics given to him. My father has taken to boasting about this – as in 'there's not an antibiotic alive that can touch George Mole'.

Tania has worked hard to turn him into a middle-class new man. But, I fear, to no avail. Since his garden pagoda accident, he has reverted to type: the *Sun* is delivered to his bed every morning by the Women's Voluntary Service, and he inevitably picks all the stodgy food items on the computerized menu form. Tania has given up reading improving literature to him, since he laughed out loud at the end of *Jonathan Livingston Seagull*.

When I arrive home, I find a heartening scene of inter-generational harmony. Mrs Wormington, my mother, Glenn and William are sitting in a circle passing the nit comb from one to the other. William has introduced headlice into our house yet again.

Ivan Braithwaite came to pick up my mother. He has recently been diagnosed as suffering from over-choice syndrome. He broke down in the washing-powder aisle at Safeway. He was observed on a CCTV camera to be acting bizarrely – walking up and down the aisle for a full 20 minutes while scribbling calculations on a notepad. He then knelt by the boxes of Persil biological tablets and wept. When my mother finally turned up to collect him, he was sitting in the manager's office, hungry and thirsty. He'd been offered tea or coffee and ginger nuts or digestives, but had, of course, been unable to choose between them.

I don't like the man, but I sympathize with his affliction. My own temples start to throb when it comes to choosing between the hundreds of shampoos on offer.

Monday, June 5

Worked on *Sty*, my pig novel. Since finishing with Pamela Pigg, I have been writing better than I ever have done before. Was P. Pigg blocking me in some way?

Tuesday, June 6

While the boys were at school and Mrs Wormington was having her feet done by a peripatetic chiropodist, I wrote 250 words of *Sty*. Should I give my pig-hero a name, or should the pig stand for struggling humanity? I need literary advice from an editor.

10 p.m. Just looked up 'Editors' on the net and found the editor of the year . . .

To: Penguin Books, Kensington

Dear Louise Moore,

Congratulations on your prestigious win. My name is Adrian Mole. I am a full-time carer and part-time novelist and dramatist (as yet unpublished and unperformed). My current work-in-progress is a stream-of-consciousness novel about a pig. I have set myself some problems – obviously, I am not a pig myself and I have no idea what pigs think about all day. May I come to see you?

I remain, madam, your most humble and obedient servant,

Adrian Mole

Thursday, June 8
Ashby de la Zouch

I am on the very horns of a dilemma. An insert fell out of Mrs Wormington's *Daily Express* today. A colourful shiny piece of A6 paper headed 'Celebrity Star Match!' invited me to scratch off the panel on an illustration of a Mercedes convertible, to reveal a picture of a famous star. I did as instructed. Slowly, as a tiny pile of metallic grey dust collected, I began to see the features of Cameron Diaz.

Mrs Wormington was looking over my shoulder. 'Oos she when she's at 'ome?' she said. (The last time she went to the cinema was to see Rock Hudson. I pray she never finds out that Rock had to steel himself to kiss Doris Day – the truth could easily kill her.) I carried on reading the instructions: 'Now, one at a time, starting with panel one, scratch the four panels alongside.' At this point, Glenn and William begged to be allowed to scratch two panels each. Glenn read further instructions aloud as William scratched. 'If you reveal a matching picture – stop scratching – you're a winner!' Alas, his vigorous work with the two-pence piece revealed Tom Cruise and George Clooney. Mrs Wormington peered at these two mega heart-throbs and pronounced them 'Nancy boys' who looked as if they 'couldn't stuff a lavender bag'.

William pronounced himself to be 'devastated' at his failure. I must stop him watching so much television; it is having a deleterious effect on his vocabulary. He has no sense of proportion. He fell off his tricycle yesterday. When I asked him if he was all right he said, 'I'm cool, Dad, I just want to get on with the rest of my life.'

The tension grew as Glenn picked up the coin. He took a deep breath and scratched away. The features of Samuel L. Jackson gradually took shape. Mrs

Wormington confused him with Michael Jackson and seemed to be under the impression that M. Jackson had actually married his pet chimpanzee, Bubbles. I tried to explain to her that the ape had, in fact, been the best man at Elizabeth Taylor's last wedding, but I could see that the ways of the modern world were beyond her comprehension.

The atmosphere was now so tense that I could feel the word 'palpable' vibrating in the air of the room. Glenn closed his eyes in silent prayer, then scratched at the fourth panel. Unbelievably, incredibly, the smiling face of Cameron Diaz appeared from among the grey filings. Our collective shout of delight brought Vince and Peggy Ludlow round from next door. 'I've won a Mercedes, Dad!' shouted Glenn and we had a collective hug, though we didn't include Mrs Wormington, who has brittle bones. I read on feverishly.

'Winners can find out what they've won right now. Just call 0906 551 1020 and listen. Have a pen ready to write down your personal claims number which you will need if you claim a prize.'

I turned the leaflet over. Glenn hadn't necessarily won a convertible Mercedes, though for at least 10 deliriously happy seconds, he thought he had. He told me later that he had fantasized in that short time about driving to school in the silver car with the hood down and gangsta rap playing on the in-car stereo. He'd parked next to the headmaster's clapped-out VW and had walked across the playground with the car keys swinging from his index finger. I had to break the news to him that he may have won other, lesser prizes, including: a weekend in Cannes with £500, a dishwasher, a set of hardwood garden furniture, or even lesser prizes such as key cases, razor sets, kitchen scissors and mixed seed packs.

Peggy read further down the leaflet and pointed out that to discover what Glenn had actually won would cost me £1 a minute, and that the average call lasted longer than 3.5 minutes.

You see my dilemma, diary? Do I fork out more than three quid, only to find that Glenn has won a packet of mixed seeds, or do I take a stand against exploitation and risk losing a convertible Mercedes?

Thursday, June 22
Ashby de la Zouch

There is great excitement in the street. Brandon Ludlow, 22-year-old soccer fan, is due home this afternoon from Charleroi, Belgium. A banner has been erected outside the Ludlows' house. It says: 'Welcome Home Our Hero'.

Brandon was arrested before the England–Romania match. Apparently, he was having a quiet meal at a pavement cafe and was talking about Tolstoy with his friend 'Mad Dog' Jackson, when a brutal Belgian policeman in riot gear thrashed him unmercifully with a baton.

Mad Dog Jackson escaped, but Brandon was restrained with a cable tie and thrown into the back of a police van, where he lay, face down, only inches from a pool of urine. When the van was full, it was driven to a police station. Brandon was pushed towards a holding cell, where he and 40 others stood until daybreak. Brandon was not allowed to phone the Ludlows, his family (and anyway, it would have been a futile exercise since the Ludlows' phone had been cut off by BT for non-payment).

Peggy Ludlow is threatening to sue the Belgian prime minister as soon as she finds out who he is. As she was preparing the party food, she said, 'Adrian, our Brandon is the only one of my kids who ain't a hooligan. Our Brandon's always been a strange kid, you know, reading books for pleasure and talking about things that none of the rest of us are interested in.'

She told me that Brandon only went to the match for research purposes. He is writing an essay about David Beckham, entitled 'God Or Idiot Savant?' He is hoping to see it published in the *London Review Of Books*.

4 p.m.
I can tell from the noise outside – car horns blaring, whistles blowing, Dobermanns barking – that Brandon has arrived home. We have all been invited to the party. Glenn and William are very excited, as they have been watching the rioting in Charleroi avidly.

In fact, they have shown more interest in the fighting on the streets than they have shown in the football on the pitch. Mrs Wormington talked to me as I ironed one of her vast, full-skirted summer frocks. According to her, certain sections of young Englishmen have always behaved like barbarians when they have travelled abroad as a group. She said, 'How do you think we managed to capture all them foreign countries? It weren't the limp-wristed brigade what done it and coloured the map pink.'

She insisted on wearing a hat to the Ludlows' party, seemingly under the impression that it was Ludlow Castle she was going to rather than the front room of a council house. I had a very interesting talk to Brandon, who is indeed a sensitive, intelligent young man. He reminded me of my younger self, before I became trapped in single fatherhood and the endless round of domestic duties (which now includes caring for a nonagenarian). Over Mother's Pride and Kraft processed-cheese sandwiches, we discussed his ordeal. Brandon said that his night in the cells was only made tolerable by the fact that a barrister had also been arrested and had happened to have a copy of last week's *Spectator* magazine on him. This same barrister kept trying to get his fellow hooligans to chant Boris Johnson's name, but few joined in and eventually he gave up and went to sleep, but only after confessing to Brandon a particularly lurid sexual fantasy that included Petronella Wyatt and Bruce Anderson.

After a heated discussion with Vince Ludlow about Mrs Worthington's habit of banging on the party wall with an orthopaedic shoe every time the Ludlows enjoyed sexual congress, I took my family home.

Sunday, June 25

Brandon came round as promised to read my manuscript of *Sty*. I dare not let it out of my sight. A lot of work has gone into the first three chapters. Brandon looked up after the first few pages and said that he thought it was a mistake to call my pig hero Lucifer, as it set up false Mephisophelean expectations in the reader. I could have done without such stinging criticism but I have to concede that Brandon has a point. While waiting for the washing machine to finish its cycle, I re-christened Lucifer and called him Peter. It is amazing what a difference this has made to the tone. It now reads like a children's book. I may subtitle it *A Farmyard Allegory*. Watch out, Harry Potter. Peter Pig is on the way!

Saturday, July 1
Ashby de la Zouch

To kill two birds with one stone, I decided to read William the rewritten manuscript of *Sty!* as a bedtime story. The political and philosophical sub-text will be beyond him, but I hoped that the narrative would grip him. After a few paragraphs, he bleated that he wanted a Noddy and Big Ears story, but I persevered.

Peter Pig lifted his porcine head from the trough and looked up at the mercilessly grey East Midlands sky. A cloud, which looked like a Boots cotton-wool ball, scudded across the aforementioned sky like a Eurostar train leaving Waterloo station.

Peter sighed and walked around the sty. The filth and mud oozed between his trotters. It was disgusting, the condition he had to live in, he thought. Why should Farmer Hogg and his wife, Pamela, enjoy the comfort of carpets and vinyl tiles underfoot while he and his fellow pigs be condemned to wading through their own excrement?

Peter looked over the sty, towards the patio where Farmer Hogg and Pamela were holding a barbecue for their friends.

The foul stench caused by pork fat dripping on Do It All charcoal briquettes drifted over to him, causing his eyes to run.

He listened to the conversations of the humans as they gorged on their buffet, which Pamela had been preparing since *The Archers* finished on the radio.

Peter watched the guests quaffing Buck's Fizz and longed to feel the liquid in his own mouth. He looked across the sty to where his fellow pigs, Antonia and Miles, were having a heated discussion about the nature of existence. Peter sighed, he was sick of philosophical debate. It was just his luck to be trapped in a sty with two intellectuals. How he craved small talk! He twitched his ears towards the patio. He strained to hear the conversation.

'Well, I'm sick of it,' said a grey-haired man called Ken, 'after all Mo's been through.'

A well-presented woman called Barbara hissed: 'Not here, Ken, there's a chap called Derek from the *Ashby Gazette* standing by the gherkin jar.'

'I won't be silenced,' Ken thundered. 'It's unmanly of Tony to stab her in the back.'

From the sty, Peter watched as Derek turned from the pickle jar, took out his reporter's notebook and edged towards Ken and Barbara.

It was at this point that William started whining about wanting a Noddy story. However, I continued with *Sty!* for a few more lines.

Another group of people provided the small talk that Peter thirsted for. From a woman in white jeans, he heard: 'We do support the comprehensive system, but our children are terribly sensitive, so.' And a man wearing wire Ray-Bans opined: 'House prices have got to come down soon. We bought ours for . . .'

Peter was in heaven. Later that night, the barbecue long extinguished, Peter looked up at the stars and ruminated on the nature of small talk. To help him sleep, he practised the art. He selected one of his favourite topics: 'Call this a summer? I can't remember the last time the sun shone.'

Within minutes, William was asleep.

Sunday, July 2

I loathe Noddy, but I had promised William, so I made up the following story.

It was Big Ears' birthday, so, to celebrate, Noddy drove his car to Toytown. The pals went from pub to pub, drinking pints of beer. Big Ears' face got very red and the bell on Noddy's hat rang like mad. When they came out of the last pub, a gang of Skittles accused Big Ears of being a pervert, and started a fight. Mr Plod was called and saw Noddy head-butting the largest Skittle.

'Hi ham takin' you to the nearest cash point,' said Mr Plod. 'Tell me your PIN number, Noddy.' But, sadly, Noddy was too drunk to remember, so Mr Plod hit him hard on the head with his truncheon instead.
Good night.

Wednesday, July 5
Arthur Askey Walk

My father originally went into hospital with fractures of the leg and various other injuries, caused when he fell off a ladder while constructing a Japanese-style pagoda for Tania, who is obsessed with all things Oriental.

He's been in hospital for months, suffering from a hospital-borne infection, and is now completely institutionalized. When he hears the food trolley arrive at the end of the ward at 7 a.m., 12 noon and 5 p.m., his mouth fills with saliva. He claims to be happy there, says he has no worries: other people pay the bills, walk the dangerous streets, get immobilized in traffic jams and do the Sainsbury's run.

Sharon Bott, the mother of my son, Glenn, works as a cleaner at the hospital. She says that, as part of an infection-control programme, her mop was taken away for laboratory tests. She said that when the mop was returned to her, 'It looked as if it had been through the mill.'

Thursday, July 6

I have just found a sheaf of poems hidden inside the panel surrounding the washbasin. They are in Glenn's handwriting. Why he feels the need to hide the evidence of a fine sensibility is a mystery to me. This house is devoted to the creative spirit. William, for instance, has a passion for making miniature gardens in old shoe-boxes. Perhaps he will grow up to be a landscape gardener like Capability Brown or Charlie Dimmock.

My favourite poem is entitled 'Why?'

> *Why?*
> Why, oh why do nice things die?
> A leaf, a flower, a humble fly?

I will have to correct Glenn on an inaccuracy in this poem. Flies are not nice. They have vile personal habits. My second-favourite poem is called 'Patsy'.

> *Patsy*
> I love the way your mouth goes up
> When you drink from out a cup.
> That Liam was no good for you
> Come to me, I will be true.
> I cannot give you mega-wealth
> But I am young, I have my health.
> Flee from London, leave your cage
> But know one thing, I'm under-age
> I can't have sexual intercourse,
> I'm chaste like that Inspector Morse.

When Glenn came home from school, I tackled him about the poem. He hung his head and blushed scarlet. 'Don't tell no one, Dad,' he said.

Saturday, July 8

My mother has called a family conference. I am the subject. My father was on the end of his hospital telephone. Others present were: Ivan Braithwaite, Tania, Mrs Wormington and my Auntie Susan, a prison warder. They are concerned that I am wasting my life. I pointed out that I am a full-time carer of two boys and a 95-year-old woman. My mother said, 'What was the point of reading all those books if all you're going to do with that knowledge is to wash and iron and cook? You might as well have been born a woman.'

Auntie Susan stubbed out her cigar and raked her fingers through her number two before saying, 'Adrian, I could get you a job in the prison library.'

To shut them all up, I promised to think about it, but the thought of being in contact with even literate prisoners fills me with horror. Tania said that, in her opinion, I had an unhealthy fixation with old people. 'Why can't you be content to do voluntary work in a retirement home? Why do you feel the need to have one living with you?' I was unable to give her an answer. When they had gone, Mrs Wormington asked, 'Who was that stuck-up bitch in the kimono?'

Monday, July 10

Next week, I go to Wind-on-the-Wolds Prison to be shown around the library. There is a part-time job available, worse luck!

Thursday, July 13
Ashby de la Zouch

My mother has just phoned in a panic, gabbling about CJD. She was once driven through the village of Queniborough on the way to a garden centre in Quorn and is now convinced that she is to be the next victim in the cluster of unfortunates to have contracted the deadly disease. She has become a hypochondriac since Ivan Braithwaite moved into our house with his mania for sterilizing the chopping boards and sprinkling Dettol on the new dog's bedding.

I tried to calm her fears but she was near to hysteria and begged me to forgive her. 'For what,' I enquired, wondering which of her parental crimes I should forgive her for. 'The cheap beefburgers I used to serve up, three times a week,' she said. 'I didn't know they were made of bits of old spinal cord and sawdust, Aidy.'

I reassured her that the beefburgers of my child-hood were so utterly disgusting that I used to surrep-titiously feed the dog with them. It would take its place under the table whenever it saw my mother drag a box of the vile things out of the freezer. Per-sonally, I'm waiting for the boil-in-the-bag cod-in-butter-sauce food scare. I must have consumed a shoal of the fish. Then there's the frozen-beef TV-dinners-for-one, which we used to consume on Sundays. That tinfoil couldn't have done us much good, either. 'It's 100% organic food for me from now on,' said my mother.

'But you don't know what to do with real food,' I reminded her. She replied, 'I've got Delia and Nigel and Jamie to help me,' as though her ill-equipped kitchen was full of celebrity chefs jostling for space.

Friday, July 14

Mrs Wormington has gone to Mablethorpe with the Ludlows. They have got an eight-berth caravan in a field near to the sea. They asked if they could take William with them but I had to say no. He is an impressionable lad and easily picks up on the

Ludlows' verbal infelicities. Yesterday he came back from playing at their house, and when I told him it was time for bed, he said, in a Louisiana accent while showing me his left palm, 'Tell it to the hand, cos the face ain't listening. Leave a message after the bleep.' Peggy Ludlow said that the *Jerry Springer Show* had been on while William had been playing on the rug with Vince Ludlow's socket set.

Saturday, July 15

I watched the *Inside Downing Street* documentary tonight. What a fine figure of a man he is. He is masterful, charming, clever and has a good head of hair. He is altogether impressive. Alistair Campbell is the man I would like to be. Mr Blair, on the other hand, seemed lacklustre by comparison. He has been transformed since Leo insisted on sharing the marital bed and Euan started hitting the bottle. In fact, Tony has undergone a feminization: his hair has turned fluffy, his voice has softened, his expression is girly, his hands move as gracefully as a geisha's. Is he on a course of hormones that will eventually transmogrify him into Toni – the first woman Labour Prime Minister? The country should be warned. We will need time to adjust to the change.

William Hague, on the other hand, is awash with testosterone lately. He'll be starting a parliamentary chapter of the Hell's Angels next if he doesn't watch his hormone levels. Does Ffion welcome this new thrusting Mussolini-like man in her bed, or is she already sleeping in the spare room, like Prince Edward's wife?

Sunday, July 16

The Ludlows have returned home with hypothermia after walking along the promenade at Mablethorpe. Mrs Wormington has been taken to hospital in Skegness. She has been wrapped in a silver space-blanket.

When Auntie Susan rang my mobile and asked angrily why I'd not turned up at the prison library as promised, I replied truthfully that I was anticipating a tragic bereavement.

Wednesday, July 19
Ashby de la Zouch

The summer weather in Mablethorpe has killed Mrs Wormington. She was a perfectly fit 97-year-old when she left my house in Ashby de la Zouch on Friday,

July 14, at 1.15 p.m. I am being specific about details because Eunice, Mrs Wormington's daughter-in-law, has just left this house after calling to collect the dead one's belongings. She accused me of sending 'an ailing woman to the east coast, to die'.

It was only after she had driven off in her Reliant Robin that I realized that she was virtually accusing me of murder. I immediately called my mother, who is an acknowledged expert on litigation (she haunts the small-claims court). She advised me to seek the advice of her solicitor, Charlie Dovecote.

It cost me £50, plus VAT, to be told by Dovecote that allowing a nonagenarian to ride a donkey in a stiff east wind may have been foolhardy, but did not constitute murder.

I found a bundle of old letters under Mrs Wormington's mattress when I stripped her bed. I was glad that the horrible Eunice had missed them.

October 21, 1917

Dear Sergeant Palmer,

I hope you are now settled into your new quarters in Ypres and that the weather is pleasant. We hear most marvellous reports of General Haig's leadership from the newspapers. I am glad that you are in such safe hands. Thank you for asking me to call you Cedric. However, I feel it is far too early in our friendship for such intimacy. We have only known each other for a year.

Yours with best wishes,

Miss Broadway

This, I presume, was Mrs Wormington's maiden name. Social intercourse was conducted with such delicacy in those days. It's no wonder that Mrs Wormington was shocked at Denise Van Outen's grubby little TV show. Even I, an admirer of the female breast, begin to tire of prime-time mammaries.

Thursday, July 20

William wanted to know where Mrs Wormington had gone. I said she had gone on a long journey to a place where she would be in peace. I went on a bit, about Mrs Wormington running up hills and picking wild flowers under the warming rays of the sun, etc. Perhaps I went too far down the pastoral path, because when William was watching Glenn clean his roller-blade boots I heard him say, 'Mrs Wormington's not dead, Glenn. She's gone to live in Teletubby Land.'

Friday, July 21

A car in which Jack Straw was being conveyed was stopped by police for speeding at 103 mph. I hope the full might of the law is brought to bear on the miscreant. I am still smarting from the tirade of abuse I received from a traffic policeman because I drove at 32 mph in Foxglove Avenue, a 30 mph zone. When I remarked, humorously, 'I'm not exactly Jeremy Clarkson,' the policeman sneered, 'No, he's taller, got more hair, and is almost certainly richer and more famous than you are, Sir.' I thought of reporting him to the Police Complaints Board, but wasn't sure if sarcasm counted as assault – though I still feel hurt by it.

Saturday, July 22

I went to see Pandora at the MP's surgery today. I wanted to talk to her about my theory that Mr Blair has secretly embarked on a course of hormones that will transform him from Tony to Toni. I reminded her that he'd recently stated that he disliked wearing a suit.

'Don't be so bloody ridiculous,' she snapped. 'Get

out and give your seat to a constituent with a genuine problem.' I pointed out that there was nobody else waiting to see her. 'Apathetic bastards,' she raged of the electorate. 'I could have stayed in London and picked up my bowling bag from Prada.'

I had no idea she'd taken up such a middle-aged, boring sport.

Monday, July 24
Ashby de la Zouch

There was a surprisingly large turn-out for Mrs Wormington's funeral this morning. I hadn't known she was a member of so many societies and clubs. There were mourners representing Amnesty International, the Fox And Ferret ladies' darts team and the Cacti Club of Great Britain. I hadn't realized she had such Catholic tastes. In the time she lodged with me, most of our conversations had been about biscuits, though towards the end of her life she spoke obsessively about the state of the Queen Mother's teeth.

William begged to be allowed to go to the funeral; I gave my permission, but warned him against talking in the church. The boy has a voice like a town crier. He let me down only once, when he asked, in the lull between a hymn and a prayer, 'Dad, why do old people smell?' The church was packed with the elderly, who failed to see the charm or humour in the boy's innocent question. One old bloke along the pew shouted to his deaf neighbour, 'He wants a bloody good hiding.' I had warned William what to expect: that there would be a box called a coffin and that Mrs Wormington would be inside it, dead. He seemed to take in this fact, but when the coffin started to be lowered into the grave, William shouted, 'You'd better get out now, Mrs Wormington.' He said later, at home, that he'd thought dead people came back to life, like Kenny in *South Park*.

At the service, I read a poem I'd written. It seemed to go down quite well – though my mother said afterwards at the funeral lunch that she thought it was gross self-indulgence on my part and should never have been torn from my pad of A4.

Requiem for Mrs Wormington
She was not a little old lady
She was six foot tall.
She didn't smile sweetly
She wouldn't play ball.
She didn't wear chiffon
Or white gloves to wave.
She lived through two wars

But wasn't called brave.
She drew her own curtains
And cooked her own dinners
She worked in a factory with good folk and sinners.
Her overdraft didn't exceed £1.50.
But she didn't get praised for being so thrifty.
Farewell, Mrs Worthington, fan of Nye Bevan
I hope you are warm again up there in Heaven.

Several people asked me the significance of 'warm again', not knowing that Mrs Wormington had died of hypothermia after holidaying in Mablethorpe.

Tuesday, July 25

Glenn and William are on holiday from school for six weeks. What am I going to do with them? I have no funds with which to entertain them. We are only one day into the break, but William has already declared himself to be 'bored'. I told him that, when I was a lad, I entertained myself with non-stop activities. But, in truth, all I can remember doing is staring out of the window and waiting for school to begin again.

Wednesday, July 26

I reluctantly drew out £50 from the building society, bought a family rail ticket and took my sons to Tate Modern. No one warned me about the vast metal spider in the Turbine Hall. William is an arachnophobe and froze with fear on seeing it. He then emitted a piercing scream. An American tourist asked me if William was an 'auditory accompaniment to Louise Bourgeois's sculpture'. I said 'no', that he was just a little boy who was scared of spiders.

Thursday, July 27

The Concorde crash is off the front pages; no British people were killed.

Saturday, July 29
Ashby de la Zouch

Ivan Braithwaite continues to be fascinated by what he calls 'working-class culture'. He has suggested that our family go to Skegness on what he calls a 'bucket-and-spade holiday'. He drivelled on about candyfloss, donkeys and 'the glorious vulgarity of the amusement arcade'. I had no choice but to say yes. I can't afford my preferred holiday – visiting literary shrines throughout the world. In fact, so far I have only visited one: Julian Barnes's house in Leicester. Though he left there when he was six weeks old.

Sunday, July 30

A boarding house has been booked: The Utopia. Bed, breakfast and evening meal will cost Ivan £13.50 per adult per night – half-price for William. Rosie has refused to go: she said she has got to attend her new boyfriend Mad Dog Jackson's graduation ceremony. He is now an MA, and his dissertation, 'Socialism, Necrophilia And Other Taboos', has provoked interest from the *Spectator*.

Monday, July 31
The Utopia

Talk about a major infringement of the Trades Description Act! The Dystopia would be a more accurate title for this Draylon hell-hole. I share a draughty attic room with William and Glenn. There is no space in which to swing a dead vole, let alone a cat. The view from the skylight is of mournful-looking seagulls with morsels of chips in their beaks. The owners, Barry and Yvonne Windermere, are ex-variety performers. I shall go mad if Barry tells me another 'joke'. Ivan and my mother think this raddled old duo are 'fabulous characters'. Personally, whenever I hear the fabulous characters phrase, I want to run – into the sea, until the cold waves close over my head.

Wednesday, August 2
wind shelter, Skegness

Glenn is sulking in the attic. He has already spent all his pocket money on the slot machines in the arcade where we were forced to take shelter from the cruel wind that blows unchecked from the Urals across the North Sea. Ivan and my mother struggled to construct a windbreak, and William, dressed in an anorak, sheltered behind it and tried to make a sandcastle, but his fingers turned blue and I had to take him into a cafe to thaw out. The place was full of shivering families eating terrible food. Ivan went on saying to my mother, 'This is an authentic working-class experience, isn't it, Pauline?' His eyes were shining with excitement. He is turned on by vulgarity. It is why he fell in love and married my mother.

My mother drew heavily on her St Moritz menthol fag with the gold-rimmed filter and said, 'Ivan, I'm no longer working class. I read the *Guardian* and buy coffee beans now, or hadn't you noticed?'

Thursday, August 3

The sun came out today. Ivan bought a kiss-me-quick-and-shag-me-slow sunhat. I saw my mother wince when he put it on, but she kept her mouth shut and feigned interest in a stick of rock shaped like a penis.

Friday, August 4, Queen Mother's birthday

Barry and Yvonne have decorated the dining room with Union Jack bunting. The little table where the condiments are normally kept has been turned into a shrine to the Queen Mother. Two candles burn either side of a lurid photograph of the aged one.

Barry met her once, backstage at the Palladium. 'What did she say to you? I asked. 'She asked me how long I'd been waiting,' he said, his slobbery lips trembling with emotion. 'And what did you reply?' I asked. 'Not long, ma'am,' he said, and almost broke down.

Unfortunately, Glenn knocked over one of the candles at dinnertime and set fire to the Queen Mother's photograph. I threw a cup of tea over it, but the damage was considerable. We have been asked to leave. Proof, perhaps, that there is a God.

Friday, August 18
Ashby de la Zouch

I have been brutally betrayed! I feel humiliated and sick! How could he have told such terrible lies to me over the past five weeks? I admired him so much. He was the type of man I would have liked to have been myself. He was a man who could cope with adversity (the death of his young wife in a car crash). A man who led other men (an officer in the Territorial Army). He was also a healer (like Jesus), and a reiki master to boot.

I would have followed him into the jungle with hardly a qualm. So confident was I that 'Nasty Nick' would win the £70,000 that I withdrew £50 from my long-term diamond deposit savings account (incurring loss of interest) and placed a personal bet with my father. It was with glee that my father phoned me at 4.45 p.m. today from his hospital bed, where he is still languishing with several NHS-bred infections, to tell me that my hero was about to be evicted from the House.

I didn't believe my father at first, diary. He once told me that I had won £7 million on the lottery. This cost me dearly. To celebrate my 'win', I rang the Lotus Flower home-delivery service and ordered the banquet special for six. On discovering my father's cruel joke, I tried to cancel the order, but ended up having an angry confrontation on the doorstep with Mr Wong, who wouldn't get back on his moped without the £96.21 he insisted that I owed him.

However, when my mother rang my mobile to tell me that she and Ivan were watching on the net, I knew it must be true. I could hear Craig's dental lisp quite clearly down the phone. The Ludlows came from next door to disclose this world-shattering news, and Vince said, 'It's a bleedin' triumph for the working class, if you ask me.' Peggy Ludlow said she'd always thought Nick was Tim Henman, who had fled to the Big Brother House in disguise in order to avoid playing tennis.

I couldn't sleep last night. Do all my heroes have feet of clay? I have only recently recovered from Mr

Aitken's downfall. I pray that Lord Hattersley will not be unmasked as the secret author of Mills & Boon romances, or that Will Self will not be exposed as a committee member of the Caravan Club of Great Britain.

Saturday, August 19

I said to Glenn today, 'Glenn, you will always remember where you were when you heard that Nick had been expelled from the House.' He looked back at me and said, 'Course I will, Dad – I was watchin' it on the telly.'

'You were taking part in history,' I said.

'What, like the Second World War?' he asked doubtfully.

'No, more like the day Beckham had his hair cut,' I said.

'You're mixin' up popular history with proper history, Dad,' said Glenn. Chastened, I went to my bedroom to start the third chapter of *Sty!* (Swine fever has wiped out the entire pig population of Britain, apart from Peter, my hero. I may retitle *Sty!* and call it *The Last Pig* instead.)

My father rang this morning and insisted that I honour the bet! Personally, I think it was a great mistake to provide hospital patients with bedside telephones. They give their long-suffering relations no peace with their incessant, peevish demands for Lucozade and boxes of tissues.

Monday, August 21

The Last Pig
Peter watched from the sty as the 4×4 drew up by the computer shed in the farmyard. He saw Farmer Brown emerge from the chemical store and greet the Sky News crew. 'Where's the last pig in Britain?' shouted a researcher. Peter rolled in the mire. He wanted to look good on camera: he was going to be famous.

Sunday, September 3
Arthur Askey Walk

Can you trust anybody nowadays? My financial adviser, Terry 'The Shark' Brighton, has been arrested by the fraud squad. Apparently, he has been operating a caravan finance scam for years. So I can kiss good-bye to my £500 deposit and my dream of owning my own Willerby Westmoreland 'van and siting it on my mother's property. True, she was hostile to my plan, saying, 'I don't want trailer trash living on my doorstep,' but I could have talked her round, in time.

I have got to leave the Gaitskell Estate before William bends to peer pressure and starts taking a laser pen to school. The Ludlows next door are going through a period of marital discord. Hardly a day or night goes by without a violent argument and the sound of a human head being banged against the party wall. I feel sorry for poor Vince. Peggy is a fearsome woman when she is roused.

Monday, September 4

The autumn term has started, thank God. William complained this morning that his school uniform is too big for him. I told him it was his own fault for refusing to try it on in the shop. But I may ask my mother to turn up the trousers. They drag on the ground and make him look as though he is a double amputee.

Vince came round this morning, begging for sanctuary. He told me that Peggy found him in bed last week with their daughter's best friend, Mandy Trotter.

'She bleedin' flung herself at me and got me zip

undone before I could stop 'er,' he whined. 'What was I s'posed to do?'

Glenn pointed Mandy Trotter out to me when we were in the Co-op. She was stacking the lower shelves. She is only four feet eleven inches tall and, though obviously over the age of consent, she looks like an emaciated child. Vince couldn't have fought very hard to keep her off his zip.

Tuesday, September 5

Peggy has been round to give her side of the story. Apparently, Mandy Trotter is pregnant with Vince's child. 'What's he see in that skinny slag?' she asked. Her magnificent bosom was heaving and her gloriously long fishnetted legs were crossing and uncrossing as she sat at my kitchen table, dropping ash on my vinyl tiles. I was speechless with desire for her.

It's time I found a sexual partner: a non-neurotic, childless, non-smoking, beautiful woman who enjoys literature, spotting Eddie Stobart lorries and housework would be ideal. Is it too much to ask that I should be allowed a little happiness?

Wednesday, September 6

I tried to understand what Mr Robin Cook was saying on the *Today* programme this morning. I think he was talking about his ethical foreign policy. However, he now gabbles his words and speaks at such a rate of knots that it is impossible to understand him. This is an infringement of my human rights as a British voter. Does Gaynor understand a word he says lately, or has she long stopped listening to her wee bearded elf of a husband?

Thursday, September 7

Ivan Braithwaite has been sectioned under the Mental Health Act! It took four policemen and a straitjacket to get him in the ambulance. His mind snapped when his laptop, his printer, his fax, his three phones, his television, his radio and his pager were all switched on at once, relaying different information.

When my mother came into his workspace and said, 'Ivan, do you want to know something?' he flipped and started smashing the place up.

Robin Cook should take warning.

Saturday, September 9
Arthur Askey Walk, Ashby de la Zouch

There are now two male members of our family in hospital: my father's infections keep mutating, and he is now the subject of a controlled drug trial. He's in an isolation unit. Quite honestly, this has come as quite a relief: visiting is strictly forbidden. It is possible to observe him through a glass panel, but what's the point of driving seven miles there and seven miles back to watch a middle-aged man puzzling over the *Sun* crossword?

Ivan Braithwaite has also been forbidden visitors. The psychiatric nurse in charge of him, a certain Steve Harper, said, 'Ivan needs a break from the family dynamic.' The family dynamic in question, my mother, is furious and spends most of the day sitting outside the locked ward telling anybody who will listen that it is 'an overload of information technology that caused Ivan's breakdown'. He'd processed 300 emails only half an hour before he cracked, she told me. I am now convinced that technology is to blame for most of society's ills.

I used to scoff at my dead grandmother Edna Mole's assertion that microwaves damage the brain, but since upgrading to a superior wattage I have noticed a diminution of brain power. It took me more than an hour to remember whether it was Shakespeare who wrote, 'He that sleeps feels not the toothache', or Sir Walter Raleigh. I spoke these words at 4 a.m. to Glenn, who has got an abscess. However, he didn't sleep but kept me awake with his groans of pain. It was just our luck not to have a single painkilling tablet in the house.

Sunday, September 10

At first light, I went to the emergency chemist and asked for paracetemol. The chemist, a child of 10, asked me if I intended to kill myself. I assured her that I didn't, and she handed over the pills. I tried to buy petrol today, but the queues were too long and there was a fight on the forecourt. Why?

Monday, September 11

Mohammed at the BP garage refused to sell me more than £5-worth of lead-free this morning. We were at school together, and our relationship has deepened in friendship over my fuel-buying years, yet he refused to help me out. How am I going to get William to school? There is no convenient public transport, and the journey is almost a mile.

Wednesday, September 13

I rang my MP, Pandora Braithwaite, to complain about the fuel crisis. She reminded me that when we were schoolchildren together we used to walk a mile and a half to Neil Armstrong Comprehensive School. I reminded her that, 'This is the year 2000, where paedophiles stalk the avenues and cul-de-sacs.' She said scornfully, 'You've obviously forgotten that sweetshop keeper who used to pretend his trousers had fallen down when we innocently asked for a gobstopper.' I asked her why she was in such a bad mood. She said, 'On the contrary, I'm in an excellent mood. I'm relieved that I'm not mentioned in Andrew Rawnsley's book, *Servants Of The People*. I was sure he was going to use that story about me and Mo and Gordon Brown in that hotel service lift at Bournemouth.'

Thursday, September 14

Glenn has come home from school with a homework project about Third World poverty. I took him to the library on the next estate on a search for information. Unfortunately, it was closed due to 'staff shortages'. I rang my mother and she brought round some statistics she'd found on the internet. I was shocked to realize that me and my boys have been living in Third World poverty for the past two years.

Glenn is relieved: he was planning to do his project on Bangladesh, but now, as he says, 'All I have to do is walk around the estate, talkin' to people, Dad.'

Friday, September 15
Arthur Askey Walk

So much for a lifelong friendship! Mohammed refused to sell me any petrol today, even though I had pushed the Montego to his garage to save what little fuel I had. I reminded him that I had stuck up for him in the playground at Neil Armstrong Comprehensive when Barry Kent went on a bullying rampage after eating too many Walker's crisps. 'I don't remember you stickin' up for me, Moley,' Mohammed said as he directed a midwife towards a pump.

I pointed out that I had advised Barry to go on a bullying-awareness course at the Off The Streets youth club. 'That didn't stop me from gettin' my fingers bent back,' he said sadly.

My mother drove up on the forecourt and joined the queue of essential users. 'On what grounds are you an essential user?' I asked. 'Have you joined one of the emergency services since I saw you last?'

'As a matter of fact, I have, in a way,' she said. 'I promised to take some of my unwanted vases to Laing Ward at Ivan's mental hospital. They've got nothing to put the visitors' flowers in.' I wondered how she would convince Mohammed that her need of fuel was legitimate, and was infuriated when she was allowed to go to the front of the queue and was served by Mohammed himself!

I made another attempt to procure some petrol for myself. Citing the time I directed Mohammed in the Nativity play, *Jesus Christ Almighty!*, and gave him the starring role. 'Yeah, yeah, and I'm still in trouble with some of the community elders 15 years later,' he said. 'I said I'd be in trouble if I played Jesus as a heroin addict.'

'You had free will, Mohammed,' I pointed out.

'No, I didn't,' he said. 'You was going through a

bad time. Your parents were splittin' up, so I dun it to help you out.'

As I pushed my car back home, I puzzled over how a man could hold a grudge for so long. A grudge so powerful that it influenced his judgement when it came to petrol distribution.

Saturday, September 16

Pandora is thinking of buying a house in the Suffolk countryside so she can escape from her constituents. It is called Oakley Park, in Hoxne village. I looked the property up on the net, and was alarmed to discover that it was the scene of a macabre double murder in 1777, when Sir Frederick Brownlow discovered his wife Felicity in bed with Fergus Bellington, a young groom.

When I say 'bed', I am using the term loosely – the lovers were actually participating in a sexual act behind the clock over the arched entranceway. As midnight struck, Sir Frederick, tormented by jealousy, chopped them into bite-sized pieces with his sword. ('It was manayee times sharpen-ed beinge much blunted by ye bones.') The pieces were then fed to the pigs. I warned Pandora that there was a curse on the house, and that anybody with the initials

F.B. came to a bad end if they so much as stepped foot into the courtyard.

'For God's sake,' she said, 'what are you drivelling on about? My initials are P.L.E.B.' She then went into a tirade, saying that idiots were clogging up the internet with uninteresting and unnecessary information.

Sunday, September 17

Battle of Britain Day: Radio 4 was dominated this morning by a dreary church service commemorating this important historical occasion. Why does the C of E allow such very terrible music to be played in its name? And why do church officials speak in such unnatural voices like aliens?

Radio 4 should have played the soundtrack of that *Douglas Bader Story*. It would have given joy to many.

Monday, September 18
Arthur Askey Walk

Life is dull after the excitement of the petrol crisis. I have been out and about doing a little panic buying of bottled water, granulated sugar, bread mix and tinned pilchards. But nothing can compare with last week's frenzy, when, for a few moments, I truly believed that civilization was at an end and that we would be back to driving a pony and trap.

I have been called to the Job Centre on Friday to explain why I filled in a form recently stating that I am not available for work and that I would like to continue to claim benefits. I have spent all day today preparing my case. I have written a manifesto. Its main thrust is that society should support its artists. Its concluding paragraph states: 'How tragic would be the loss to the nation if a great work of mine were to remain unwritten due to the banal necessity of clocking on as an assistant warehouseman, e.g.'

Tuesday, September 19

At 1 p.m., I was contacted on my mobile by my mother, who screamed, 'Drop whatever you're doing and start queuing for petrol now!'

As I scrambled into my car, I shouted the news to the neighbours in the street. A convoy, stretching 30 cars long, soon formed behind me. By the time we got to Mohammed's garage, we were more than 100 strong and had a police escort. Mohammed's jaw dropped when he saw me leading the convoy on to the forecourt. He was just about to take his wife panic buying in Iceland – she had heard that toddler-sized disposable Pampers were in short supply. I now feel slightly ashamed of myself for getting caught up in the hysteria, but I need my car. I'm too sensitive to be a full-time pedestrian. The non-car-owning public are unpredictable, their voices are loud and their tempers are uncertain. I feel safer in my car with my Abba tapes and Radio 4.

Friday, September 22

I presented myself at the Job Centre at the appointed time, 10.30 a.m., and was surprised to be taken immediately through to an interview suite by a personable young woman called Jane Doxy. She was neatly turned out in a navy skirt suit and a white shirt. The outfit would, in my opinion, have benefited from high heels, but no doubt Jane enjoyed the comfort of her Gucci-copy loafers.

I'd had the foresight to take a copy of the *Guardian* with me, to impress on Jane that I was an intelligent and literate person. Though, when I saw the *Daily Mail* in her bag, I wondered if I had done the right thing. She had read my manifesto with great interest, she said. However, she (and the department) felt that my writing was 'only a hobby' and that 'the government was not in the game of subsidizing my leisure interests'.

She gave me two telephone numbers to ring. The first was that of Eddie's Tea Bar. Eddie himself answered. The job was assistant caterer in Eddie's cafe, which was a trailer parked in a lay-by next to the cement works. I asked what my duties would be. Eddie growled, 'You'd be doin' all sorts, fryin' burgers, changin' the Calor Gas bottle, 'n' stuff like that, for £3.60 an hour.' Under the watchful eye of Jane Doxy, I then rang the second number. A gentle pensioner called Mrs Banbury-Pryce answered, and said that she needed somebody to take her six dogs out twice a day for a walk.

I start at Eddie's on Monday. I just knew that, with my soft heart, I'd end up helping Mrs Banbury-Pryce with the fastenings on her corset and cutting her toenails.

Sunday, September 24

Woke at 5 a.m. to find that a small earthquake had shaken the East Midlands. A few dogs barked, but tragically for the local media nobody was killed.

Monday, October 2
Eddie's Tea Bar, Cement Works, Leicestershire

I am on my break and am sitting on a white plastic chair, writing on a matching picnic table. I am surrounded by lorry drivers and motorists. It is only 11.30 a.m., but I am already exhausted. I have been on my feet since 5 a.m. (though, to be strictly honest, and at the risk of being labelled 'pedant', I did sit down in the car during the journey here).

Eddie and his third wife, Sandra, were already here and the urn was warming up, as were the deep-fat fryers and the griddle. Eddie and Sandra seem to have fat running through their bloodstreams. Their hair, skin and pores seem to be clogged with it. Eddie said to me, as he gave me a huge wrap-around apron, 'You'll never shake off the stink of the fat, lad. It makes it 'ard to get a woman outside the trade.' All Eddie's wives have been in the frying business, apparently. I reassured him that I was not actively seeking a woman at the moment, and told him that I was due to start a course at the adult education centre in Leicester called 'Living Without A Partner'. He looked at me, pityingly, and asked quietly whether I had 'somethink wrong under yer clothes'.

I reassured Eddie that I was made as other men were made, but that my heart had been broken a few times recently and needed time to recover. Eddie lifted the spatula off the sizzling bacon slices and said, 'I get bad headaches if I don't have a bit of sausage-hiding once a day, don't I, Sandra?'

Sandra tucked a strand of oily hair behind an ear and said, ''E was on a box of Nurofen every 24 hours when I went in the General to have my veins done.' Eddie shook his head and gazed into the middle distance where the lorries were parked, obviously reliving the horrors of sexual deprivation.

I phoned my mother to ask how the child-care arrangements had gone this morning. She said, 'Badly. I can't get up and come to your house at five every morning. I'm falling asleep at the wheel.' I pointed out to her that day nurseries don't open until 7 a.m. and begged her to continue. She said bitterly, 'I blame Tony Blair and Jack Straw for this. Why should grandmas have to be dragged in to look after their grandkids, eh? I've already served my sentence with you and your sister.'

She made me and my sibling's upbringing sound a joyless business. I asked how Ivan was doing in the mental hospital. 'He's developed an aversion to all things technological,' she said. 'A male nurse used an electronic Ronson to light a patient's birthday cake and Ivan had to be sedated.' I wondered if Ivan 'techno' Braithwaite would be capable ever again of coping with the modern world.

Tuesday, October 3
Ashby de la Zouch

D. H. Lawrence, my literary hero, enjoyed working with his hands and reputedly took a pride in his jam-making. I, too, have discovered the small joys of manual labour. I like to think that D.H. would have been proud of me as I serve up a bacon 'n' egg sandwich to our first customer, Les, who was driving an Eddie Stobart lorry full of mineral water from Liskeard to Dundee. Though I say it myself, Les's sandwich was a work of art. The bacon was succulent, the egg was cooked sensitively, so as to prevent yolk leakage, and the bread was as white and soft as a newly hatched maggot. I was quietly pleased when Les pronounced it to be 'champion'.

Wednesday, October 4

Couldn't sleep for wondering about the necessity of hauling mineral water from Liskeard to Dundee. Scotland is awash with the stuff.

'Living Without A Partner' has been cancelled. I was the only one to turn up.

Thursday, October 5
Eddie's Tea Bar, Cement Works, Leicestershire

Working in Eddie's has given me a unique glimpse of how capitalism works. Eddie goes to the cash-and-carry and buys catering packs of bacon, beefburgers, white sliced bread, ketchup, etc., and then uses me at £3.60 an hour to convert the ingredients into food items that sell for 200% profit. Eddie does not have a computerized till. His is strictly a cash business. There is a notice on the trailer wall next to the peeling Samantha Fox poster: 'Please do not ask for a receipt, as refusal often offends.'

He keeps the coins in an old Cadbury's Luxury Biscuits tin. It offends my sense of order to see the coinage jumbled up together, but it works well enough. Banknotes are kept in Eddie's apron pocket. I suspect that Eddie pays little tax or VAT, though he is vociferous enough on the subject of social security cheats. 'They should be took to a island somewhere in the North Sea an' left to fend for themselves,' he said this morning. 'Though,' he added compassionately, 'I'd give 'em a packet of seeds an' a spade.'

Eddie's biscuit tin is the proletarian equivalent of a Cayman Islands tax shelter. All it lacks is financial advisers and accountants. Eddie's wife does his 'books' while watching the omnibus edition of *EastEnders*. It's a weekly ritual, apparently.

The lorry drivers provide another facet of globalization. Some truckers have travelled three days to haul Romanian fridges to Bolton, England. Others have taken gerbil food from Bury St Edmunds to Hamburg and returned with a cargo of Hamburgian carrots, which they've dropped off at a warehouse in Stowmarket, Suffolk. This is madness.

As I serve each trucker, I make a point now of enquiring as to his ultimate destination and the nature of his load. I have thus come to the conclusion that capitalism is no way to run the world's economy – it is inefficient and it exploits workers such as myself.

I put this argument to Eddie as I was scraping the

griddle clean with a spatula. He profoundly disagreed with my analysis and said, 'If you carry on shoutin' for revolution, Moley, you'll find yerself outta a job so far yer stupid Birkenstock shoes won't touch the bleedin' ground.'

Friday, October 6

William and Glenn are both away from school because their hair is infested with headlice. I rang Eddie on his mobile and told him that I wouldn't be in today, as I would be preoccupied with banishing the nits from my boys' heads. Eddie said, 'Me an' the missus was up all night scratching our soddin' bonces as if they was scratchcards. You should examine yer own 'ead, Mole.'

Glenn and William sat me at my desk and aimed my anglepoise lamp on to my head. There were so many nits in my hair that Glenn said, 'You could fill Wembley Stadium with 'em, Dad.' He is going to watch the England–Germany match tomorrow with a group from the school. They are doing a project on English historical monuments and he is hoping to bring a few blades of grass back to paste into his project folder. Though, as the headmaster said in his email to me, 'Glenn's head will be examined by myself

in the morning, and if evidence is found of headlice
or their progeny, in the form of unhatched eggs, he
will NOT be allowed to board the coach to Wembley.'

I was up most of the night going through Glenn's
hair with a fine-tooth comb. Eventually, at 3.30 a.m.,
I cracked and shaved his head. I used five disposable
razors. He looks decidedly thuggish, but at least he
was allowed on to the coach.

Saturday, October 7

Glenn returned victorious with a plastic seat, a square
foot of turf and one of Kevin Keegan's chewed-up
fingernails. The boy will go far.

Sunday, October 15
Ashby de la Zouch

Pandora rang me today and sought my advice on
whether or not she should confess to having smoked
cannabis at Oxford. 'Why are you asking me?' I said.
   'You're the voice of middle England,' she snapped.
'You're a perfect barometer of public opinion.'
   I resented her implication that I was a dull provin-

cial, but at the same time was pleased and flattered that my opinion was being sought. I advised her to keep quiet in the matter of her drug-taking, and warned that a confession would almost certainly jeopardize her ultimate ambition of becoming the next-but-one prime minister. She rang off after saying, 'You are right, Aidy, I must keep the *Daily Mail* on my side.'

Monday, October 16

The shadow of headlice infestation continues to fall across our house. What more can I do to exterminate the vile creatures? My mother went to the hairdresser's on Saturday, and her stylist, Sebastian, fled in horror to the colour-mixing room after spotting a colony of them nesting at the nape of her neck. She is furious with me, and claims she hasn't been so humiliated since the wire from her Gossard bra poked out of her wedding dress at the registry office when she married Ivan Braithwaite. Even my father, who is still in an isolation cubicle at the general hospital, has nits. What is going on?

I told Glenn that I suspect foul play: 'It's obvious that a foreign power, possibly Iran, has introduced a virulent form of nits into this country in an attempt to demoralize the population and destabilize the pound.'

Glenn shook his head in a pitying way and said, 'Go an' lie down, Dad, an' put a wet towel on yer 'ead.'

Tuesday, October 17

I read the following article in the *Independent* today: 'Dr Pandora Braithwaite, the junior minister for fish, admitted in a *Newsnight* interview with Jeremy Paxman last night to having smoked cannabis during her time at Oxford. To a direct question posed by Paxman, "Have you or have you not smoked dope?" Braithwaite smiled and answered, "Have you, Jeremy?"

'Paxman snapped, "I'm not here to answer the questions, minister, you are." Braithwaite said, "Okay, yes, I did, we all did. What's more, I thoroughly enjoyed it. It's what got me through the work."'

I now predict terrible things for my love. Her position as a minister of the crown is surely untenable.

Wednesday, October 18

The whole country is talking about Pandora. According to a report in the *Guardian*, the demand for cannabis in Oxford has skyrocketed.

Thursday, October 19

I returned to work at Eddie's Tea Bar today, and couldn't help but notice that many of our trucker customers were scratching their heads. Are the nits being transported throughout Europe? How long will it be before they have taken over the world? At 7 p.m., Glenn phoned my mother, and told her to come round quickly. I explained my nit theory to her, and after listening for an hour and a half, she sent for Dr Ng.

Friday, October 20

I am calmer now. Dr Ng prescribed Prozac and a course of aromatherapy. He said that I was suffering from stress. I told him about my unhappy childhood, and he was very understanding. Though I heard my mother vehemently denying it: 'He was a very happy little boy,' she told the doctor. 'Until he got older and started reading Dostoevsky and that bleddy Kafka!'

Pandora has sent me a get-well message, and suggested that I recuperate by reading Lord Archer of Weston-super-Mare's latest volume. She later phoned and told me the astonishing news that, far from being vilified for her drugs confession, she is being strongly tipped for promotion.

Saturday, October 21
Ashby de la Zouch

Last week Pandora was climbing the rungs of the snakes and ladders of life. This week she is sliding down a python's back (so to speak). The papers today are full of pictures of her cat, Maurice, who had to be rescued by the RSPCA on Thursday night after neighbours heard piteous miaowing coming from Pandora's flat in Pimlico. Unfortunately, she was on a fact-finding mission with Keith Allen in Ayia Napa at the time of the cat's rescue. An RSPCA spokesperson said: 'Dr Pandora Braithwaite may be charged with the neglect and cruelty of an animal. Maurice had not been fed for five days and was in an emaciated condition.'

I phoned Pandora's mother, Tania, for the inside story and she told me that Maurice's computerized Feed-A-Pet feeding bowl had developed a fault and had refused to open up and feed the ravenous beast. Some of the headlines were harsh: 'Pan's pet starved alone', 'Drug MP's cat horror', and 'Pan's pussy shock'.

In my role (unpaid) as Pandora's adviser on Middle England, I rang the House of Commons to offer my help. Unfortunately, she was not able to take my call as she was in emergency talks with Alastair Campbell. I left a message with her private secretary, Nigel Hetherington: 'Tell her to make a large donation to the Cat Rescue Mission.'

Nigel said: 'How very, very original. Thank you for your extremely naff idea, Moley.'

It still rankles with me that Pandora chose Nigel to be her right-hand man rather than me. Okay, so he may have three degrees – in management, business and fashion – but I feel that he lacks a certain *je ne sais quoi*. I am extremely experienced when it comes to dealing with the media. In 1993, for five months I was the *Ashby Bugle*'s poetry correspondent (unpaid) until the editor was sacked for gross insubordination (throwing an empty vodka bottle at the proprietor). Unfortunately, the new editor was obsessed with sport and turned my weekly column into a 'Spot The

Ball' competition, to the detriment, in my opinion, of Ashby de la Zouch's cultural landscape. William is not eating. I suspect he is seeking attention.

Sunday, October 22

Millbank released a photograph of Pandora and Maurice today, together with a condemnation of computerized feeding bowls. Pandora is calling for an inquiry into their reliability. She has vowed to use a cat-sitter in future. When asked about her relationship with Keith Allen, she said: 'Mr Allen and I were in Ayia Napa on a fact-finding mission. We were investigating the swamping of the British Consulate by penniless British youngsters demanding their airfare home.'

Monday, October 23

The police in Nottingham are now strolling about in the city centre with guns. How long will it be before Ashby de la Zouch rings to the sound of the Kalashnikov? Surely we are on a slippery slope.

Tuesday, October 24

Eddie rang today to complain that I haven't turned up for work. I explained about my childcare problems during half-term. He said: 'I'm tryin' to run a bleedin' caff 'ere. I don't give a toss about yer private life, Mole.' This is typical of Britain's and Eddie's attitude towards children. It's no wonder that three of Eddie's offspring are currently enjoying custodial sentences and that one, Shane, is dancing with the Royal Ballet.

Glenn has begged to be in charge of cooking in future. I was happy to pass on the Mole apron. I hadn't realized that he was interested in the culinary arts.

Wednesday, October 25

William's appetite has picked up. Glenn has bought Jamie Oliver's *Naked Chef* book with the money he has made guarding the cars of the social workers visiting the estate.

Friday, October 27
Ashby de la Zouch

Ivan Braithwaite is home from the mental hospital and is now confined in the box room at Wisteria Walk. My mother is acting as his nurse. I say 'acting' because she is most ungracious about her new role. I overheard her talking on the phone to her brother, Pete, who lives in Norwich. It was a self-pitying monologue which I reproduce here, though it gives me no pleasure . . .

'When I married Ivan I expected my life to change. As you know, Pete, Ivan is upper-lower-middle-class and he promised to stretch my horizons, but the only horizons I've seen lately have been the view from the fourth floor of the mental hospital and the vista of the back of my own back garden. I've blown it, Pete. I've turned into a bleddy nursemaid. I'm looking after our Adrian's kids as well, while he's at work.

[Pause]

'No, he's not paying me! He bought me a bunch of forecourt flowers last night and then complained because I'd given the kids lobster nuggets and oven chips for their tea instead of the stupid health stuff he'd brought round in the morning. They're growing lads, Pete. They need more than a few beansprouts and a lump of tofu. Anyway, I'd better go. I'm sorry we've not spoken for over 20 years, Pete, but Mum did promise me her charm bracelet when she died and your wife, Yvonne, had no right to claim it and wear it on her fat wrist at Mum's funeral.'

[Pause]

'No! Mum promised it to me, Pete!

[Sobbing]

'She hated Yvonne. She used to call her Nixon . . .

[Pause]

'. . . because of her five o'clock shadow, that's why!

[Pause]

'Oh, I'm sorry, Pete, I didn't know that Yvonne had died recently. How recently?

[Pause]

'Yesterday! Oh, my God! Oh, Pete. That's awful!

[Pause]

'So, you'll send me that charm bracelet in the post, will you, Pete? Remember to register it.'

At this point the call was disconnected at the Norwich end.

Saturday, October 28
The Dome, Greenwich

I am sitting here in Harry Ramsden's, waiting for Glenn and William, who are in the queue for the Body Zone. The waiting time is an hour and a quarter. When I suggested an alternative – that we visit the Prayer Zone, which did not have a single visitor – Glenn said, 'You go in an' do a prayer, Dad. Me and Will'll catch you later.'

The boy is getting to be more assertive by the day. He has already taken over the cooking at home and this morning I found a note in a milk bottle on our doorstep: 'No milk today. Gone to the Dome. Cheers milkman, Glenn Bott-Mole'. How long has Glenn had a double-barrelled name? And why is 'Mole' second? Glenn Mole-Bott has a much more refined ring to it.

The Prayer Zone was still empty. The woman vicar in the pastel tracksuit was obviously grateful to see me and hear my religious views. I told her I had recently become a tree worshipper and asked if there was an organization I could join. She looked through her index of the *Book Of World Religions*, without success before saying, 'The Liberal Democrats may be your best bet.'

Sunday, October 29

The scenes at St Pancras station were pitiful last night, as desperate East Midlanders milled around on the concourse before setting off on their detours around the broken rails of Midland Main Line.

Monday, October 30

I woke at 3.30 a.m. to find that a twister was spiralling down our street. Several wheelie-bins were overturned and a lousy, stinking tree demolished my shed.

Tuesday, October 31
Ashby de la Zouch

Pandora's weekend home, Lock Keeper's Cottage, on the banks of the river Severn, has been flooded out. She had to be rescued by a fireman in a Canadian canoe. The rescue was filmed by *Midlands Today*. Apparently, she and a 19-year-old youth called 'Scottish Sandy' had been marooned for a day and a night in Pandora's bedroom. According to her, Sandy had been stacking sandbags against her doorstep when the torrent overtook them and they were forced to flee upstairs. When asked by Julia Snoddy, *Midlands Today*'s weather correspondent, why Pandora had not alerted the emergency services earlier, the controversial MP replied, 'I knew how busy they were and did not want to add to their workload.'

Asked to describe her ordeal she said, 'It was hell. I ran out of Marlboro Lights and I'd left my Prada bag on the sitting-room floor. It has been totally ruined by the floodwater.' She told Ms Snoddy that she would be pressing Mr Prescott, the flood supremo, for financial assistance towards flood defences in the Severn–Trent area. 'It is time our rivers were lined with concrete,' she said. 'It would be terribly sad to lose the bulrushes and the wildlifey things, but we are living in a new era and cannot afford to be sentimental about nature.'

She pointed out that various retail outlets could be built on the concrete banks of the Severn: 'Starbucks coffee shops would bring cappuccino to our neglected countryside areas,' she said.

Pandora has always hated the countryside: on our nature rambles with the school, she would wear dark glasses, saying, 'All this green makes me utterly, utterly sick.' Lock Keeper's Cottage was furnished in New

York style. The blinds were kept permanently down. In fact, they were nailed to the sills.

I sincerely hope that Pandora does not achieve her ambition and become the first female Labour prime minister. During many private conversations with her, she has confided in me that she would be quite happy to see the fens covered in decking, Dartmoor replaced with Astroturf and the Lake District equipped with escalators to make it easier for the disabled. My mother claims that Pandora was only joking, but I'm convinced that her contempt for the English country-side is genuine.

Wednesday, November 1

My literary agent, Brick Eagleburger (who has failed to sell any of my novels, television series, radio plays or epic poems), got in touch with me today after a period of two years. Somebody in Wolverhampton – a certain Jim Smith – is keen to publish *The Restless Tadpole*, my 592-page prose poem about a tadpole's journey from the early days of frogspawnhood to the dying moments of old frogdom. It charts the events of the creature's life and draws parallels with events in my own, though I did not include my divorce, as I couldn't find out from any amphibian handbook if frogs went through a form of divorce, or if in fact they stayed faithful to the same partner.

Glenn has just informed me that 'frogs are at it day an' night, Dad, with anythink that turns up'.

Brick Eagleburger said that Jim Smith had sent a fax saying, '*The Restless Tadpole* is a lyrical lament for the past glory that was the English countryside. I was moved to tears by the frog's violent death under the wheels of a German juggernaut.'

Brick said, 'The guy's payin' zilcho spondoolicks but the exposure's godda be good for ya.' I asked for the name of Jim Smith's publication and was told it was *Frog Weekly*.

It touches me greatly that so many people care so deeply about frogs that they can be bothered to fill in the subscription form and fork out nine quid a year. Personally, I can't bear the loathsome slimy creatures.

Sunday, November 12, Remembrance Sunday
Ashby de la Zouch

I was the only one on the BP garage forecourt today to respect the two-minute silence.

Monday, November 13

Brick Eagleburger is beside himself with excitement. He is convinced that his Floridian postal vote will secure the presidency for Gore. He may well be right. If Gore wins by one vote, Brick plans to take the credit. He has booked a full-page advertisement in *The Stage*. It says:

> Brick Eagleburger, theatrical agent, specializes in weather girls, celebrity chefs and animal acts, including the world famous Billy the Seal. Mr Eagleburger's postal vote determined the outcome of the American presidential election. New Artistes always welcome. 25% commission. Tax and investment advice included.

I phoned Brick, and asked when he and I could meet to discuss my writing career. At 33, I am already too old to be eligible for the Young British Writers' Award. Why does nobody arrange competitions for the young middle-aged? It is sheer prejudice. Just because we are beginning to lose our hair and suffer from occasional sexual dysfunction, it does not mean that our literary faculties are clapped out. Brick told me in his hideous ungrammatical style, 'I don't got no windows, Adrian.' He said he was having trouble with Billy the Seal, who had developed a serious cocaine habit after working in a circus in Dublin, where he came under the malevolent influence of Declan Tourette and his amazing foul-talking dog. Within seven days, poor Billy was snorting a serious quantity of the evil white powder. After a fortnight, he was seriously dependent on Tourette for his supply. Within three weeks, Billy's career was almost over, his nostrils were seriously damaged and he could no longer catch or throw a ball with his nose.

Fortunately, Brick caught him in time and packed Billy off to a secret animal rehabilitation clinic in Milton Keynes. There, together with other damaged animals, Billy broke his expensive habit and cleaned himself up.

Tuesday, November 14

My life is incredibly boring, but today took the biscuit: absolutely nothing happened. I got out of bed. I made scrambled eggs. They were neither good nor bad, but sort of in between. I walked to the newsagent's, where I was just in time to see a man with a beard (a stranger) buy the last *Guardian*. I could tell from his accent that he wasn't from these parts. I think it is disgusting that people are allowed to buy goods willy-nilly, regardless of where they live, thus depriving the locals of vital supplies. I said as much to my mother. She said, 'Are you seriously suggesting that people should be prohibited from travelling from one area to another? Are you, in fact, advocating a type of postcode apartheid?'

I didn't know what to say to her. The truth was that, once again, I had reacted to a minor setback in a manner that was entirely inappropriate. Several people have commented that I should see a therapist. However, the waiting list to see an NHS therapist is two years and it would break my heart to fork out £25 a session to find out that there is nothing at all wrong with my personality or emotional make-up.

Wednesday, November 15

I have just emerged from the front room of a Jungian therapist called Dave Mutter. I sat on his pink velour sofa and cried about my grandma's Yorkshire puddings for 55 minutes.

Thursday, November 16

I rang Dave and begged him for an urgent appointment. I am seeing him this afternoon.

5.30 p.m.
I told Dave about my recurring dream – that Gordon Brown visits me at night and begs me to help him with the economy. Dave is my only friend.

    God, diary, I think I may be a little in love with him!

Saturday, November 18
Ashby de la Zouch

Dear diary, I must confide in you a most terrible secret. I am desperately in love with my therapist, Dave Mutter. Not sexually. Absolutely not sexually. Not in any way sexually. Dave is not an especially attractive man: try to imagine Yul Brynner with an overactive thyroid, a grey ponytail and a high-pitched voice. I think you'll agree that he doesn't excite homoerotic fantasies. My love for Dave is pure and strictly platonic. He fills my daytime thoughts. I live only for my next appointment with him. I long to tell somebody. I need to speak his name aloud, but who can I trust to keep my secret? Perhaps I should see another therapist and confess to him/her.

Monday, November 20
Eddie's cafe, the lay-by

I thought up the following poem whilst cleaning the deep-fat fryer at the close of business today. It is a foul, foul job but Eddie bribed me with £25, which will help to pay for an extra session with Dave.

> *Poem to Dave*
> Dave Mutter, Dave Mutter
> His name is so charming.
> My passion for him though
> Is slightly alarming.
> For 55 minutes
> Two sessions a week
> I sit on his sofa
> In anguish and speak
> Of my heartache and longing
> And alienation
> From family and friends
> And the rest of the nation.

Tuesday, November 21

Brick Eagleburger has sent my epic poem, *The Restless Tadpole*, to a certain Geoffrey Perkins at BBC TV Centre. I asked Brick which department Mr Perkins worked in. Brick said, 'The guy's head of suckin' comedy.' I angrily pointed out that *The Restless Tadpole* is an entirely serious dramatic work written in the tradition of the Icelandic sagas.

Brick said, 'Listen up, Adrian, I flicked through the suckin' manuscript of *Tadpole* and I godda tell ya I almost peed my suckin' pants, it's so funny.' Brick carried on, 'My favourite scene is when the tadpole is lying in Marilyn Monroe's garden pond and it overhears Arthur Miller talking crap about Tolstoy.'

I have always known that Brick Eagleburger is a philistine; however, he is now totally misrepresenting me and my work.

Wednesday, November 22

In my session tonight I asked my beloved Dave if it was normal to recite the Lord's Prayer before crossing the road. He raised his eyebrows slightly and fiddled with his ponytail before replying enigmatically, 'Normal is as normal does.'

What does this mean? Dave is obviously my intellectual superior. I am not worthy to be his client.

Thursday, November 23

I have engaged the services of an additional therapist. This will enable me to talk about Dave for 55 minutes non-stop twice a week. My new confidante is called Anjelica House. She is middle-aged, that's all I can remember about her. I am seeing her tomorrow after work.

Friday, November 24

Anjelica has explained to me that my love for Dave Mutter is nothing more than what is called in the mental health trade 'transference'. She is a wonderfully empathetic woman and I think I may be a little in love with her.

Geoffrey Perkins is wild about *The Restless Tadpole*. He wants to cast Dawn French in the title role.

Monday, November 27
Ashby de la Zouch

Today is only the first day of Ramadan, yet Mohammed at the BP garage is already in a bad mood due to the fasting laws imposed on him by his religion. In a normal day at work, he would eat three packets of cheese-and-onion crisps and a KitKat or two. I remarked to him that he could do with losing at least four stone in weight. To my astonishment, he burst into an angry denunciation of my character and appearance, ending up with, 'You should take a good look at yourself in the mirror, Moley. You've got enough hair sprouting out yer nostrils to weave a mouse's shoppin' basket. And you look five months pregnant.'

I apologized at once for my rudeness. I tried to explain that my therapists, Dave Mutter and Anjelica House, were encouraging me to be honest during social intercourse. This seemed to exacerbate his anger, but thankfully he was diverted from giving me another tongue-lashing by a strident female motorist complaining about the lack of toilet paper in the ladies'.

As I walked across the forecourt, I pondered on our conversation. From where did Mohammed get his image of my nasal hairs being woven into a mouse's shopping basket? And what was his reference to my looking five months pregnant about?

Tuesday, November 28

I took off my clothes and examined myself carefully in the wardrobe mirror this morning. My front view is quite nice. My shoulders are slightly stooped, my pectorals are perhaps lacking definition, but I am still above average in the looks department. However, my profile leaves a lot to be desired and, yes, Mohammed, my old schoolfriend, you spoke the simple truth: in profile, I do look five months pregnant. My belly, once a discreet concave, is now distinctly convex. How did this happen without my noticing?

I am shocked to discover that my son, Glenn, is keeping what he calls a top secret dairy. He has also written on the cover in barbed-wire writing. 'Open This Dairy At Your'e Perul'. I was very tempted to find out what the boy had written about me, and had I been able to prise the lock off without it being detected I may well have found out.

Wednesday, November 29

Can anybody tell me why we British export our beef to France and why the French export their beef to Britain? I have asked many people, but nobody has been able to provide me with a satisfactory answer. I had a session with Dave Mutter tonight after work. I told him about Mohammed's remark about the mouse's shopping basket. Dave said he found Mohammed's imagery to be 'extremely disturbing'. He suggested that Mohammed seek professional psychiatric help.

I am pleased to report that my fixation with Dave Mutter is over. He is simply a dull baby-boomer with a Minnie Mouse voice and an out-dated ponytail. However, Anjelica House, my second opinion therapist, is a truly magnificent woman. Why did I not appreciate the attractions of late-middle-aged women before? How come I have never noticed the beauty of their crows' feet or the delicious way their upper arms sag when they plump a cushion?

Midnight
Pandora has just rung to find out if my father has recovered from his hospital-borne infection yet. I told

her that he was still being barrier nursed. She was delighted: she wants to use him to illustrate a point about privatized hospital cleaning services. Before she rang off, she hinted that the row between John Prescott and the French Minister Dominique Voynet was in fact more of a lovers' tiff! So, were they slaking their lust while the world festered on its axis? If so, we, the world's population, should be told.

Thursday, November 30
Ashby de la Zouch

My mother has signed up to be an Earth Watch volunteer. She is hoping to count birds migrating over a lake in Kenya. Frankly, I am disgusted. My mother is abusing a worthy conservation project. To my sure knowledge, she has never shown the slightest interest in birds, Kenya or counting. She is obviously hoping to get a free holiday. Earth Watch should be informed: she can't even count. The figures for migrating Kenyan birds could be hopelessly confused for years to come. This could lead to stress and trauma amongst ornithologists and their possible premature deaths.

I confided in Glenn my worries about the orphans of the Kenyan ornithologists. He furrowed his brow:

'Why are you worryin' about somethin' that 'asn't 'appened yet, Dad?' I had no satisfactory answer. Later, my therapist, Anjelica House, asked me precisely the same question. Perhaps I should give her £25 fee to Glenn. At least it would keep the money in the family, and save me the trouble of driving to Mrs House's house, thus avoiding the attendant parking problems and the embarrassment of overhearing Mr House urinating in the downstairs cloakroom.

Friday, December 1

I rang my mother's house this morning, and was astonished and outraged to learn that she was in Paris! Ivan Braithwaite told me she had gone to the hotel where Oscar Wilde died 100 years ago this week. How dare she swan about on the Eurostar when people are starving? It is disgusting. Especially when it is me who is the Wildean expert. Few who saw it will ever forget my depiction of Lady Bracknell in the sex-swap performance of *The Importance Of Being Earnest* at Neil Armstrong Comprehensive School in 1982.

Brick Eagleburger has asked his solicitor, Peter Elf, to take a civil action against the American government.

Brick is now convinced that his postal vote has been violated. Apparently, Mr Elf was reluctant at first to take on the US, being more used to doing a little light conveyancing in the Hampton Wick area.

Saturday, December 2

I have resigned from my position at Eddie's Tea Bar. The work was very unfulfilling and I never properly came to terms with the constant smell of rancid fat on my clothes. Eddie took my resignation with equanimity. He said, 'I knew you weren't cut out for the caterin' industry the first time I clapped eyes on yer. You ain't got the wrists for it.' I asked him in what way my wrists were deficient. He answered, 'They gotta be flexible for the butterin' and the fryin', an' your wrists are about as flexible as a lump of bleedin' coal.'

I related this conversation to Glenn as we prepared lobster nuggets for our dinner. He asked, 'What's a lump of coal?' I said, 'It was a piece of black, shiny rock that we used to set fire to and burn in fireplaces.'

He laughed long and hard. The lad thinks that central heating has always been around. He probably thinks that Jesus had a double radiator in the manger.

Sunday, December 3

The rabble on the estate have formed themselves into a choir and are going from door to door demanding money for singing a few discordant notes of Slade's 'Merry Christmas Everybody'. Those of us refusing to hand over a few silver coins are threatened that our wheelie-bins will be pushed down the road and possibly overturned. I phoned Lee Bush, our community policeman, but could only get his voicemail.

Monday, December 4

William has been chosen to play third shepherd in the school Nativity play. I went to Habitat tonight and bought him a new tea towel for his headdress. Only the best is good enough for my son.

Wednesday, December 6
Ashby de la Zouch

William still believes in Santa Claus, and he nagged me to take him to see 'Santa' abseil down the side of Debenhams last night before ceremonially entering his grotto on the third floor. We stood at the front of the crowd and when Santa landed with his beard askew and his red suit in disarray from the harness, William shouted, 'Santa, will you bring me a PlayStation 2 for Christmas.' Santa replied, 'Of course I will, lad.'

I could have killed the old git. How am I going to get the money together to buy a PlayStation? They are £200. And, anyway, there are none to be had in the land. Shall I tell the truth to William and inform him that the abseiling Santa was in fact a grizzled member of The Rockettes, the Leicestershire Rock Climbing Club (a person who has no authority to make promises about Christmas presents), or do I wait until December 25 to see the disappointment on the kid's face?

My extended family is in turmoil about Christmas arrangements. Nobody knows where to go on Christmas Day, Boxing Day or New Year's Eve. Only one thing is certain: I will not be entertaining anybody in this house. I can't even afford the Barbie Advent calendar that William has set his heart on. I asked Mohammed in the garage if I could buy one for half price, being, as we are, halfway through the month. But he refused! How mean can you get? He said he would put the Barbie Advent away until next year and get the full price. So much for goodwill to all men.

Thursday, December 7

Tania Braithwaite gave out a grudging invitation to us to join her at The Lawns on Christmas Day as we stood in adjoining queues in Safeway. She said, 'Come round if you've nowhere else to go.' A quick glance into her trolley reminded me of her turkeyless and chocolateless attitude to the festivities. Soya products predominated, and there were a dozen bottles of elderflower cordial. No wonder my father refuses to get better and shake off his hospital-borne infection. He planned to spend Christmas Day with Tracy Lintel, his barrier nurse. The balloons, crackers and party-poppers are in the hospital sterilizer even as I write.

Friday, December 8

Pamela Pigg rang today. She said, 'I can't get you out of my mind, Aidey.' Glenn overheard (her voice is rather shrill). He said darkly, 'You'd 'ave to be outta your mind to go out with her again, Dad.'

164

Pamela has got a new job working with tramps, although she calls them the single homeless. She told me that there are several vacancies in the night shelter. She added that she thought I had all the qualities needed to work with such unfortunates.

'Yeah, you ain't got no sense of smell,' said Glenn. He was alluding to my recent failure to detect a packet of five-week-old prawns which I'd inadvertently left in the car next to the heater. Others were gagging as I drove, to my considerable bewilderment. Perhaps I should go to the Leicester Royal Infirmary and ask for a nasal efficiency test.

Saturday, December 9

My mother has covered the front of her house in a life-sized flashing-bulb depiction of Santa on his sleigh. It is vulgar beyond belief. Her front garden is dominated by cardboard cut-outs of Posh, Becks and Baby Brooklyn. Each has a wire coat hanger and tinsel halo about their heads. 'They are the holy family of the year 2000,' she said. However, I predict that she will soon tire of the crowds who collect after dark every night. Somebody has already stolen Brooklyn's manger.

Monday, December 11

Brick Eagleburger is suing Peter Elf, his solicitor, for failing to protect his rights as an American Postal Voter, after Elf refused to act for Brick, saying he was 'a bit rusty' on the intricacies of US constitutional law.

Tuesday, December 12
Ashby de la Zouch

Crowds continue to flock to gawp at the Posh, Becks 'n' Brooklyn tableau in the front garden of my mother's house. Encouraged by the attention, she has added three kings bearing gifts. The first king (Tom Hanks) is dangling a Prada carrier bag from his cardboard fingers. The second king (Danny DeVito) is offering Baby Brooklyn a Gap fleece. The third king (Sylvester Stallone) is holding a bottle of Calvin Klein aftershave.

I asked her where she got the life-sized cardboard cut-outs. She said she had a contact in the film business. I predict disaster. The neighbours are furious because they can't park their own cars outside their own houses. The police have been called twice and warned my mother she could be charged with breaching the peace. Citing his fragile mental health, Ivan Braithwaite, my mother's most recent husband, has gone back to live with his ex-wife Tania, at The Lawns.

My mother, Ivan and Tania all claim that this is only a temporary and platonic arrangement. But I'm not so sure. When I drove Ivan away from Wisteria Walk with his overnight bag and his laptop, I saw him visibly relax. And when he stepped into the spacious, white-carpeted, quiet hall of the Lawns he was almost in tears.

Tania greeted him with a glass of elderflower cordial and a homemade mince pie. Playing quietly in the background was a Charlotte Church CD. It was hard to decide which was the most sickly: the cordial, the mince pie or the trilling of Miss Church. I was glad to get out. As I closed the front door, I overheard Ivan say to Tania, 'It's been absolute hell, Tania.' I was alarmed to hear her reply, 'You're home now, Ivan.'

Wednesday, December 13

My poor father, he knows nothing about the new arrangements at The Lawns. Tracy Lintel, his barrier nurse, said through her mask, 'He mustn't be exposed to any emotional trauma, it could kill him.' Adding, 'He's in line for the Longest-Stay Patient award.' I promised not to tell him that his latest wife was once again living with her ex-husband. And that his ex-wife was riding roughshod over several laws of the land.

Thursday, December 14

I had to forge the following note from Santa tonight. I laid it on William's pillow before I put him to bed.

Dear William Mole,
   I have been watching you all year, and have been pleased with your behaviour. However, I am sorry to have to tell you that my elves have failed to manufacture enough PlayStation 2s, therefore you will not find this item on the sofa on December 25.
   Yours,
   Santa Claus, Greenland

   P.S. 2,000 elves have received redundancy notices.

   He cried for half an hour because Santa had written 'yours', instead of 'love'. He is a very sensitive boy.

Friday, December 15

The Nativity play started 15 minutes late because one of the parents, a certain Mrs Lucy Morgan, tried to smuggle a video camera into the assembly hall. She refused at first to give it up, citing the Freedom of Information Act. The headmistress, Mrs Parvez, cited the European Privacy Law. Several *Guardian* readers got involved in the ensuing debate. Some were on the side of Mrs Morgan, others sided with Mrs Parvez.

William was, quite frankly, a most disappointing shepherd. He dropped his sheep and in a bored manner began to kick it around the stage. At one point, the kicked sheep came dangerously close to toppling the baby Jesus (a swaddled Action Man) from his cradle.

Glenn commented as we waited for William, 'Mr Blair says it's all right for parents to smack their kids now, Dad.'

I said, 'I can hardly beat William for being a bored shepherd, Glenn.'

He replied, 'If he'd had Jesus outta his cradle, I'd 'ave jumped on the stage an' given him one myself.'

Friday, December 22
Ashby de la Zouch

Another night out! This time at Neil Armstrong Comprehensive, my alma mater, to see Glenn in *The Holiday Play*. In my day, it was simply called the Nativity play. In the 1982 performance, Pandora was a mesmeric Mary. Several men in the audience fainted during Jesus's protracted forceps delivery.

I sat next to Mohammed, whose daughter Raki was in the cast, playing a glue-sniffer running away from an arranged marriage. To my considerable consternation, Glenn had been cast as a homeless abuser of alcohol. The production was confused, because the children had not been given lines or told where to stand or, in fact, when to make their entrances and exits. This led to severe overcrowding on the stage at times, and necessitated Mr Billington, the young drama teacher, to issue loud instructions that could clearly be heard above the horrible din of the school orchestra.

Roger Patience, the headmaster, sat next to the stage with his head in his hands. The action apparently took place in a night shelter. A pregnant female called Marie turned up with her 'partner' Joe and asked the social worker in charge for sanctuary. What Marie actually said was, 'I gotta lie down cos I'm 'aving a kid an' the filth is after me for nickin' a swaddlin' cloth outta the everythin's-a-pound shop.'

To which the social worker/innkeeper in turn replied, 'Ya gotta be jokin', ain't ya? There ain't no bleedin' room, it's holiday time, you shoulda booked.' Here, Joe intervened: 'Don't dis my chick, man.' Then Glenn made his entrance and proceeded to give an alarmingly realistic depiction of a man who had consumed several bottles of methylated spirits.

A female derelict/angel came on and shrieked, 'I just seen a bright star appear in the east. It weren't there before. It done my 'ead in.' Mohammed's daughter then entered, sniffing on a tube of Bostick (empty, I hope). I felt Mohammed shift uncomfortably in his seat. I lost track of the dramatic events after that and turned my attention to the programme. I noticed that Pamela Pigg had been credited with 'facilitating research on the homeless'.

When I next looked back at the stage, Raki was giving an improvised speech about the difficulties of being a radical feminist growing up in a fundamentalist Muslim household. Mohammed muttered, 'If she thinks she's gettin' them Timberland boots for Christmas, she's gotta nuther think comin'.'

Mr Billington gave a speech at the end, thanking the children for their 'enthusiastic grasp of improvisational techniques'. He wished us all a 'merry holiday'.

As we walked to the car park together, Mohammed said, 'Moley, why don't they do a proper Nativity play no more?' I said that it was felt in some circles that it was inappropriate in a multicultural school.

Mohammed laughed and said, 'What kinda circles? Crop?'

We went for a Christmas drink at the King's Head. I asked for a cheese roll, but was told that they only do Thai food now. I didn't fancy slurping on a bowl of noodles as I drank, so I ate nothing. As a consequence, I felt slightly drunk when I got home and phoned Pamela Pigg and asked her out. She accepted eagerly, saying, 'I've longed for this moment.' After putting down the phone, I cursed the two pints of shandy I had consumed earlier.

Monday, December 25

Christmas Day has been blighted. A tragedy has befallen my family. Last night, my mother was arrested and charged with GBH.

The tableau of Becks, Posh and Brooklyn in her

front garden drew huge crowds of gawpers. Bail was refused because she gave a policeman a Chinese burn on his wrist when he tried to dismantle Brooklyn's crib. The policeman is undergoing trauma counselling, and is expected to be on sick leave for two months.

2001

Monday, January 1, 2001, 1.30 a.m.

I saw the new year in alone. Glenn has gone to a fancy-dress party at his mother's house. Rather disturbingly, he went as Hannibal Lecter. William is spending the weekend with his mother and her new husband, who are on honeymoon in London.

I hope my ex-wife and her new spouse can forget their sexual passion for long enough to pay proper attention to William. The lad has had two major disappointments in his life lately:

a) Santa's broken promise to bring him a Sony PlayStation 2;
b) Santa's broken promise to bring him a Barbie Plane.

As midnight struck, I reopened the bottle of sparkling Chardonnay I failed to finish on Christmas Day, but the sparkle had gone out of it. So I poured it down the sink.

As I wrote the numbers 2001, I was transported back to a classroom at the Neil Armstrong Comprehensive, and a lesson on 'the future' given by Miss Elf, the humanities teacher. By 2001, according to Miss Elf, the world would be one big, happy, cappuccino-coloured family. I remember her drawing this frontier-less world. How the chalk dust flew!

Miss Elf was a passionate and committed teacher. In fact, not long after I left school she was committed to the High Towers mental hospital, following a doomed staff-room romance with Podgy Perkins, the games master. He was married with seven children, all boys. (Interestingly, all the boys' names began with G.) Strange what the memory throws up.

Anyway, Miss Elf envisaged that, by 2001, there would be no hunger in the world and that everybody would have access to clean water and a flushing toilet. She drew a typical 2001 world family on the board, using a fresh box of coloured chalks. They all had brown skin and wore white, shiny body-suits with pointy shoulders. Attached to their ankles were tiny jet engines. These devices enabled the 2001 family to fly like the birds. Though, as she pointed out, inter-continental travel would necessitate many refuelling stops.

Perhaps it is a good thing that Miss Elf is gibbering behind the high walls of an institution. She would be heartbroken to know that her Utopian vision is as far away as ever, and that Israel and Palestine are still arguing the toss.

New Year Resolutions

1. I will try and secure the services of Dame Helena Kennedy in a bid to get my mother out of prison.
2. I will persist in trying to get my serial killer comedy, *The White Van*, made by the BBC.
3. I will try to be less judgemental. Perhaps Jeffrey Archer is innocent. Perhaps the Dome was worth a billion pounds.
4. I will look into the Buddhist religion with a view to becoming a cohort. I have always had a horror of treading on insects. Ants in particular.
5. I will attempt to fall in love with a suitable woman this year. One that doesn't cry a lot or use too much blue eyeshadow.
6. I'll teach my son's the proper use of the apostrophe.

Tuesday, January 2

Pandora is back from Israel, where she claimed to be on a fact-finding mission about Jerusalem. I remarked on her tan. She said, 'Yeah, I managed to get

a few days off in Eilat, swimming with the dolphins.'
How I envy Pandora's physical prowess! I would find
it difficult to swim with goldfish.

I asked her if she was any nearer to achieving her
medium-term goal, that of becoming foreign secretary. She tossed her treacle-coloured hair back and
said, 'It's acknowledged by those that count – Ian
Hislop, Auberon Waugh and Andrew Rawnsley – that
Robin's got to go. The man is now totally incompre-
hensible. How poor bloody foreigners understand his
mad gabble, God only knows.'

Monday, January 8
Ashby de la Zouch

I woke at 7.32 a.m. with a headache. Thankfully, the
boys were still asleep, so I was able to dress and attend
to my toilette in peace for once. I did not wash
my hair in the shower. The friction caused by the
massaging of the shampoo into the scalp is putting a
strain on my follicles and causing hair loss. I was
pleased to use one of those shower caps, which I have
collected from hotel bathrooms over the years.

The reason for my tension headache must be linked
to the fact that Pamela Pigg stayed last night. Or, at

least, most of the night – she left my bed at 4.30 after sobbing for an hour and a half, incidentally smearing one of my finest pillowslips in blue eyeshadow.

Our date went well, considering that Pamela had a heavy cold and kept asking the waiter for more paper serviettes in which to blow her nose. We talked about our on/off relationship, and Pamela blamed our sexual incompatibility for the fact that it was mostly off. She said she was willing to try again, and told me she had forced herself to read *The Joy Of Sex*, and then been astonished at the range of things on offer. She made it sound like the Argos catalogue.

After a protracted argument with the waiter about the bill (I refused to pay £3.50 for the extra services), we left the restaurant arm in arm. In the car on the way home, she placed her right hand over my left. It was difficult changing gear, but I didn't complain.

When we got home, Glenn was still up, doing his humanities homework. He was stuck on one question: 'Name three members of the shadow cabinet, apart from William Hague.'

Unfortunately, neither me nor Pamela could help him out. When Pamela went to the lavatory, Glenn glanced at her and whispered, 'You must be desperate, Dad.' In the lull before Pamela's return, I remembered Ann Widdecombe. When Pamela returned, smelling of Poison, and with newly applied pink lipstick, Glenn tactfully withdrew and went to bed.

I put on a Beethoven CD, the 1812, and tried to dim the lights, but the dimmer switch refused to work, so we sat under the glare of 500-watt spotlights. After a little conversation about my mother in prison, we went upstairs. Pamela apologized for her sports bra and utility-type knickers, saying that her best underwear was in the wash. I said it didn't matter, but, in truth, I was very hurt. She had known about our date for over a week. Surely that was enough time in which to hand-wash a few delicate scraps of lace and satin, and dry them on the radiator?

She commented on the fact that the spots on my back had almost cleared up, then turned the bedside light out and lovemaking commenced. The problems began when she requested that, for safety's sake, I wear two condoms, one on top of the other. God knows, I tried, diary, but by the time I'd got the first fitted, the second had got lost in the bed.

The second problem was that Glenn shouted through the party wall, 'For God's sake, Dad, 'urry up an' get it over wiv.' Which made Pamela roll over to her side of the bed, where she lay with rigid limbs and a set jaw. I tried to relax her by talking about my father's treatment for his hospital-borne infection, but she started to cry. And nothing I said would stop her.

An hour later
Glenn has just come into the kitchen, angrily flourish-
ing the used shower cap and shouting, 'Tell that
Pamela Pigg, to take 'er female condom 'ome wiv 'er
in future.' The lad obviously knows nothing about
the female anatomy.

Saturday, January 13

My ex-wife Jo-Jo has faxed me to ask if she can take
William with her when she returns to her home in
Lagos, Nigeria. For what she's called 'an extended visit'.

I faxed back immediately, c/o The Hempel Hotel
in Craven Hill Gardens, London. (She is rolling in
money – her new husband imports 'cattle prods' from
Turkey. One dreads to think to what purpose the prods
are used. I suspect that cattle don't enter the equation.)

Dear Jo-Jo,
I will cut immediately to the chase. No, you cannot
take William back to Nigeria with you. He is extremely
happy living in the small town of Ashby de la Zouch.
The culture shock could kill him. If, when he gets to the
age of reason, he wants to 'discover his roots', I will help
him to do so. But he has told me that he wants to
continue to attend Mrs Claricoates' reception class,

where he is excelling at colouring-in and computer studies. Besides, he has a school trip to Fylingdales Moor in Yorkshire, planned in February.

Incidentally, I am surprised at your choice of new husband. William tells me that the man has never heard of Pokémon cards, and that he was unable to name the individual members of Steps. He sounds an unworldly man.

How could a sophisticated woman like you saddle yourself with such a dolt? I cannot but fear for the longevity of your marriage. As you will recall (perhaps fondly), when we were man and wife, we used to talk in bed for hours about world and current affairs.

Anyway, Jo-Jo, I'm afraid you must return to Nigeria without William.

I remain, yours, as ever,

Adrian

Sunday, January 14

I received the following fax this morning:

The Hempel, Craven Hill Gardens, London.

To Adrian Mole from Mrs Jo-Jo Mapfumo.

Thank you for your fax. I am, of course, disappointed

that you will not give your permission for William to visit Nigeria with me and my new husband, Colonel Ephat Mapfumo. My family in Lagos are most anxious to meet him. He is, after all, my first son and is accordingly held in high esteem by them.

I found your remarks about my husband offensive in the extreme. He is far from being a dolt. He was educated at the Sorbonne and Sandhurst. He plays the piano, violin and oboe, collects contemporary African art and has written an acclaimed book: *The Coup – A Post-Colonial Alternative To Democracy.*

As to our own marriage, I do not recall our conversations in or out of bed 'fondly'. My recollection is that you talked at length about three subjects: 1. Your unpublished novels; 2. Dostoevsky; 3. The Norwegian leather industry. I realized that our marriage was a mistake five minutes after the wedding, when you accused me of exhibitionism, because I chose to wear my traditional tribal dress.

Yours,

Mrs Jo-Jo Mapfumo

P.S. If you will not allow William to visit Nigeria, then my family must visit him in Ashby de la Zouch. I will proceed with these arrangements as soon as I return to Lagos.

I admit that on the day of our wedding I was taken aback when I saw Jo-Jo enter Leicester Register Office. She had told me that she was going to wear 'traditional dress'. Therefore, I was expecting white lace and a veil – not a riot of pattern and primary colours. In her tribal turban, she stood 6 ft 3 in. tall. She towered over me. We looked ridiculous as we lined up in front of the registrar.

I distinctly heard Pandora (the best man) whisper, 'Talk about a *folie à deux*.'

Monday, January 15

At the last count, there were 213 members of Jo-Jo's immediate family. There's no way I can give even minimal hospitality to 213, as Nigerian custom demands. It may be easier if William went to them. Perhaps during the summer holidays.

Tuesday, January 16
Ashby de la Zouch

Clive Box, the postman, banged on the door at 6.15 this morning, which startled me out of my sleep. For some reason, I keep expecting to be raided at dawn by the police, though I have done absolutely nothing wrong. Clive had no proper letters for me, only a multicoloured envelope that informed me in fat multiple exclamation marks that I had won £1,000,000.

I said irritably, 'Couldn't you have just put it through the letterbox?'

'Sorry,' Box mumbled, 'but I wanted to ask you summat important.'

Behind Box's uniformed back, I could see that the estate was covered in frost. Box looked longingly at the radiator in the hall. I asked him in and shut the front door. He put his sack of letters on the floor and blew on his hands. He looked at the self-portrait of Van Gogh that hangs on the wall.

'Who's that? Your granddad?' he said.

'No!' I said. 'That's Van Gogh, whose genius went unrecognized in his lifetime. He only ever sold one of his paintings before he died.'

'I'm not surprised,' said Clive Box, after looking more closely at Gogh's haunted expression. 'He's an ugly bugger.'

The hall is tiny. We stood in too close proximity. I led the way into the kitchen and plugged in the kettle. Box sat at the table and said, 'You're an educated man, ain't you, Mr Mole?'

I replied that I was a bit of an autodidact.

'I ain't interested in your sex life,' he said, 'but I've seen them letters from book clubs, so I've chosen you to 'elp me out. Do you speak French?'

'*Mais oui*,' I replied.

He took out a sheet of paper from his uniform pocket and pushed it across the table. ''Ow do you pronounce this?' he asked, stabbing with a stubby finger at a word in block capitals in the middle of a paragraph. I looked at the word. I wasn't familiar with it.

'CONSIGNIA.' I said it out loud, slowly. 'Con-sig-nia.'

He then said it many times, like a toddler learning the word hippopotamus. 'What does it mean?' he asked eventually.

I told him that I had no idea. I read the paper in front of me. It said that the Post Office had given itself a 'modern and meaningful title'. And that the words, 'Post' and 'Office' no longer described the work that this organization did.

Box looked at me with bewilderment in his eyes. 'So I ain't a postman now?' he said.

'Apparently not,' I replied. 'You're a *consignée*.'

Wednesday, January 17

On the train to London to visit my mother in Holloway, I noticed that that ticket collector wore a badge that said 'Roger Morris, Revenue Protection Officer'.

My mother was in good spirits. She has made friends with her cellmate, a woman called Yvonne, who is in prison for not having a TV licence. Yvonne's defence – that she never watched BBC1 or BBC2 – was thrown out by the court. My mother pointed her out across the visiting room.

Yvonne saw us looking at her and blew my mother a kiss.

My mother blew one back!

I said to my mother, 'You and Yvonne appear to be very fond of each other.'

She looked me in the eye and said, 'Yes, we are very, very, very fond of each other.'

I took a closer look at Yvonne. She looks like Diana Dors, the black-and-white-film star.

I stumbled through the prison gates – has my mother taken up lesbianism, as she once took up badminton and feminism? And, if she has, will she tire of it, as she so quickly tired of aforementioned hobbies?

Saturday, January 27
Ashby de la Zouch

It is Glenn's birthday on Friday. Yes, the lad will be 14. Mohammed, whose brother works for Midland Mainline, gave me two Eurostar vouchers to Paris last week saying, 'You use 'em, Aidy. I daren't leave the country. I'm frit that immigration won't let me back in.'

I said, 'Mohammed, you were born in the Leicester Royal Infirmary maternity unit, you have a strong Leicester accent, you cried when Martin O'Neill left Leicester City Football Club. Nobody could possibly question your English nationality.'

'Oh, yeah,' said Mohammed cynically. 'And who was the only kid to be stopped at Dover when we come back from that school trip to France?'

I cast my mind back to that heady day when I became a European. I will never forget my first sight of *la belle France*. As the ferry prepared to dock, Miss Elf gathered her class of 30 around her on the vomit-stained deck and said, '*Mes petits enfants, regardez vous la belle France, la crème de la crème, de la Continent.*' (Or words to that effect, diary. My French is a little rusty, as I rarely have occasion to use it.)

We lost precious time in France because Barry Kent tried to leap from the ferry on to the harbour wall before the docking procedure was quite finished. He wasn't in the water long, but by the time the gend-armes had finished their paperwork, a couple of hours had been lost.

On the coach, Miss Elf announced that, due to Barry Kent's foolhardy leap, there would now be no time for the planned visit to the war graves cemetery (we were doing a class project on First World War poetry). A few of the more sentimental girls wept, I recall, though Pandora was not among them. 'Instead,' she said, 'we will sample French bread and French coffee, and we will visit a market and observe the care with which the French choose their fruit and veg-etables.'

When I returned home late that night, my mother was waiting for me in the car park of Neil Armstrong Comprehensive. As I stepped off the coach, I said to her, '*Maman*, I have seen and tasted paradise. You must throw away your Maxwell House and your Mothers Pride thin-sliced and embrace the *baguette* and *café au lait*.' I can't recall her exact words of reply, but they were said with a snarl.

Anyway, diary, what I said to Mohammed was, 'It was your own fault you got stopped by immigration at Dover – you were openly smoking a Disque Bleu fag and you *were* only 12 years old.'

Sunday, January 28

My plan is to take Glenn to Paris for his birthday. It is to be a surprise, so my preparations must be made behind his back. Tonight, I washed and ironed his least gangsterish-looking clothes and hid them in my wardrobe. There is nothing I can do about his hair or the Buffy The Vampire Slayer tattoo he's now got on his wrist, but with luck it will be cold and he'll have to roll down his sleeves. I'm looking forward to showing him the Louvre – he's a very lucky boy; I was 26 before I saw that the Mona Lisa wasn't worth the wait in the queue.

Tuesday, January 30

I was checking and re-checking my travel necessities list tonight. Two Eurostar tickets, travellers' cheques, Nurofen, map of Paris, French/English dictionary, passports, umbrella. There was something missing. Then the realization hit me like an orange thrown by a toddler in a supermarket trolley: GLENN DOES NOT HAVE A PASSPORT!

Wednesday, January 31

Pandora has refused to help fast-track a passport for Glenn. I phoned Keith Vaz MP, but there was nobody available to take my call.

Friday, February 2
Ashby de la Zouch, Leicestershire

I was sitting in the kitchen with a chicken noodle Cup A Soup this evening, waiting for *The Archers* to begin, when to my astonishment I heard my name mentioned on Radio 4. I turned up the volume and listened in growing horror to a 'trail' of a television programme featuring a man called Adrian Mole, a former offal chef whose family home is in Ashby de la Zouch.

This TV Mole has a mother called Pauline and a father called George. This cannot be mere coincidence – somebody has published my life and is exploiting it for commercial reasons. I immediately rang my agent's solicitor, Peter Elf, and left a message. The BBC must be prevented from broadcasting this series. Surely I have intellectual copyright on my own life?

I was unable to concentrate on *The Archers*, and

thus missed a strand of an important storyline: will Kate go back to South Africa with her black lover and take her first-born child?

Saturday, February 3

Several people, including Pandora, have rung up to enquire about the Mole TV series. Pandora was out-raged, though I could tell that she is rather flattered that she is being played by Helen Baxendale.

Monday, February 5

I rang Greg Dyke's office at 7 a.m. this morning, but the slug-a-bed was not at his desk. Do we licence-payers award a full-time salary to a man who appar-ently works part time? It would appear so.

Mr Elf warned me against taking out an injunction against the BBC. He said, 'It would be a David and Goliath situation.' I pointed out to him that little David was in fact the victor against the giant Goliath. Elf replied, 'In my opinion, David struck lucky with that stone. Goliath obviously had a very thin skull.'

*

Tania Braithwaite brought last week's *Radio Times* around this morning. Inside, was a 'film-set diary' purporting to have been written by a bloke calling himself Adrian Mole. This Mole bloke was also upset that his life was being exploited.

A friend of Tania's in publishing had told her that an old hack called Sue Townsend had been trying for years to publish the secret diaries of Adrian Mole, claiming that they were fiction. She showed me a piece of the manuscript. I read with increasing astonishment as details of my private life were revealed. How does this woman know so much about me? Is she tapping my phone? Has she bugged my house? Tania said that Townsend grew bitter after going on an Arvon poetry course led by Adrian Henri and Roger McGough, where Henri told her that she was not a poet and never would be after she handed in a poem called 'A Contemplation Regarding Earwig Defecation':

> How to measure earwig poo?
> How to know how much they do?
> Are there scales to measure it
> Those tiny piles of earwig shit?

Townsend then made a hysterical denunciation of modern poetry and ran out of the class and down to the river. She threatened to throw herself in unless Adrian Henri sent her earwig poem to Bloodaxe with a recommendation that they commission a thick volume of her verse. Adrian Henri came to the opposite bank and shouted across the river, 'Throw yourself in and give us all a break.'

Townsend has hated all men called Adrian since that day. A. A. Gill is another of her obsessions. Is she the reason my own literary endeavours have come to nought?

Tuesday, February 6

Leicester-born painter Adrian Hemming has fled the country after hearing that Townsend is an admirer of his work. 'I heard that she was planning to buy one of my "wave" pictures and hang it in her bathroom,' he said from his hiding place. 'I must protect my name.'

Sunday, February 11
Ashby de la Zouch

Does the psychological medical establishment formally recognize Ikea rage? I think I suffered three separate episodes of it today. The first came in the car park, when a small child, who appeared to be in charge of parking, turned me away from a disabled space. I showed him a photocopy of a letter from my doctor, which clearly stated that I was suffering from a medical condition, but he indicated that I must back out of the space and allow an invalid carriage driven by an old git in a neck brace to drive in. Dr Ng's letter:

Dear Mr Mole

Further to your many visits to the surgery this week. Your blood test results have returned from the lab and show beyond doubt that you are not suffering from HIV, BSG or MRSC. Your heart, kidneys, liver, lungs and brain are functioning normally for a man of your age. You are, however, suffering from severe hypochondria. I have discussed your case with my colleagues, Drs Singh and O'Neil, and they are satisfied that my diagnosis is correct. May I suggest that you examine other areas of your life for the cause of your unhappiness.

Dr Ng

P.S. In future, please do not visit the surgery or request a home visit unless you are certain that you are suffering from a life-threatening illness.

The second Ikea rage attack occurred in the Storage System section, when Glenn disputed my measurements for the run of Billy bookcases I'd planned to install in the living room. 'I'm tellin' yer, Dad, you ain't gonna get three of 'em against that back wall,' he said. We faced up to each other as weary shoppers tramped by. I was aware of Glenn's testosterone pumping through his teenage body. 'I will not have you questioning my calculations,' I roared, and Glenn stormed off with his tail between his legs. I eventually caught up with him in Bathrooms, where he was standing in a shower stall, sullenly examining the fixtures. In the warehouse, he silently helped me to lug three flatpack Billy bookcases on to a trolley. If he'd been in the army, I could have charged him with dumb insolence.

My third attack came in the 10-deep queue, when the woman customer at the till insisted on opening the five boxes containing a fitted wardrobe and proceeded to count the screws. My temples pulsed with irritation so much that I feared I would suffer an aneurysm and be carried out in a flatpack coffin.

Monday, February 12

I rang Pandora at the Commons and asked her to translate the Swedish instructions for assembling the Billy bookcases. As I waited for her to fax them to me, I marvelled at her courteous and helpful tone. Then I remembered: she will be fighting a marginal seat in May, and every vote will count, including mine.

Tuesday, February 13

I have tried and failed to assemble the Billy bookcases. There is obviously something in my genetic make-up that prevents me from holding a screwdriver in one hand while sinking screws into a hole in a plank of wood with the other. I now divide the world into those who can and those who can't assemble Ikea furniture. Can list: Paul Daniels, Frank Bruno, William Hague, Madonna, Princess Anne, Glenn Bott. Can't list: Peter Mandelson, Caroline Aherne, Prince Charles, Sir Edward Heath.

Wednesday, February 14, Valentine's Day

Not a single card. Not one. Nothing. Glenn received 11. They are standing proudly on top of the two Billy bookcases he assembled last night. The third didn't fit.

Thursday, February 15

A Valentine's card arrived this morning from Pamela Pigg. The cheapskate had affixed a second-class stamp. Inside, she had written, 'Let's try again.'

Sunday, February 18

I organized my library tonight, using my own idiosyncratic alphabetical system. So, the first book on my Billy bookcases was A. A. Gill's *Collected Works*. The last was zzz's, *The Insomniac's Handbook*.

In between, of course, were the tomes penned by the masters and mistresses of literature. How I longed to join them!

I went to bed after loading the washing machine with a pile of mixed colours but woke only an hour later worrying about the escalating tension in Iraq. Glenn keeps asking me awkward questions about Britain's role in the protection of the no-fly zone. Such as: ''Ow can it be called protection, Dad, when old people an' little 'uns got killed?' He is an unsophisticated boy and can't quite grasp the subtleties of the situation.

I tossed on my pillow, haunted by past humiliations: the time my mother came to a parents' evening at Neil Armstrong Comprehensive wearing yellow tights; the day my father and I sat on a bus together and he began to sing 'If I Ruled The World'; my wedding night, when I couldn't unfasten the cord of my pyjama trousers and my bride, Jo-Jo, was forced to cut it with the scissors on her Swiss army knife; my screams brought the night porter to our room, having been summoned by an irritable executive next door.

At 4.10 a.m. I gave up trying to sleep and went downstairs. I sat at my desk in the living-room alcove and found myself beginning the first sentence of a new novel. I don't have a title yet but I am rather pleased with the first page.

Chapter 1

Larry Topper blinked through his owl-like glasses as the public school, The Academy, hove into view. He turned to his guardian, Uncle Edward (his parents were both dead, killed by a bomb whilst on holiday in Iraq). 'I say, Uncle Ted,' piped Larry, 'I rather think I'm going to be jolly happy here.' Larry's glance took in the topiary which littered the large, vibrant green, well manicured, soft underfoot, lawns. Uncle Ted's kindly eyes twinkled like fairy lights before the fuse blows.

'I should hope so, young sir,' Ted rumbled in his voice which sounded like the distant roar of a bomber taking off.

Uncle Edward crunched his antique car along the gravel drive until it came to rest at the main entrance where a bored-looking boy stood smoking a St Moritz menthol cigarette. This was Brett Longshank, head boy and aristocrat who was a star of the rugger field and a genius in the classroom.

Larry gawped in awe at Brett's exquisite air of nonchalance. 'I say, Uncle,' he said, 'what a spiffing role model that fellow is.'

Uncle Ted's brow furrowed and looked like a ploughed field after several horses had dragged a plough over it.

'That's Lady Nancy Longshank's son,' he said disapprovingly. 'And I happen to know that he is addicted to crack cocaine. Keep away from him, Larry, d'you hear me? Keep away from him.'

Monday, February 19

I may give Larry magical powers. I could have an entirely original bestseller on my hands!

Tuesday, February 20

Pamela Pigg is hounding me with romantic, indeed sexually explicit, text messages. I texted her back and asked her to stop, but her ardour seemed only to intensify. Her last message came at 2.15 a.m. She wrote: 'U R 4 Me I No u Luv Me 2'.

I have decided to call my new novel *Larry Topper, Boy Wizard*. I have emailed the first page to Brick Eagleburger, my agent.

Wednesday, February 21

Dreamt that Gordon Brown was prime minister. Received a text message from Brick. It read: 'JK Rowling, you aint. But stupid U R'.

Sunday, March 11

Ashby de la Zouch

Vince Ludlow, my next-door neighbour, has got a new job. He calls himself an Animal Incineration Operative. He is uniquely qualified for this gruesome employment, having served several sentences in youth custody for arson, and actively disliking animals, claiming, 'They spoil the countryside.' He is the only person I know who is hoping that the foot-and-mouth crisis worsens. He is eagerly awaiting a state of emergency to be declared. He is planning to buy his council house on the overtime he's earning.

I was disturbed to hear that he was in the Lamb's Head car park on Saturday night selling cheap cuts of beef from the back of his van.

Monday, March 12

Peter Mandelson sounds increasingly like Joan of Arc. One can practically see the burning faggots under his feet. I saw him on the news a few days ago, handing out apples to schoolchildren in Hartlepool. He looked vaguely sinister. I was reminded of Snow White, whose simple, trusting nature was taken advantage of by the hag at the window proffering Cox's Pippins.

Pamela Pigg's surname has been causing her considerable distress. A woman in Sketchley's openly sniggered when Pamela gave her name. She made a crass joke about foot-and-mouth and cloven hooves. Pamela fled the shop in tears and drove to my house, where she distracted me just as I was about to finish the first paragraph of my latest novel, *Krog From Gork*. I made Pamela a cup of the dandelion tea she is so fond of and tried to listen sympathetically as she recounted the many humiliations she had suffered due to her unfortunate name. However, my thoughts kept straying to *Krog From Gork*.

As Pamela sobbed at the memory of her first day as a trainee teacher, I mentally composed the second paragraph of Krog . . .

Krog climbed to the brow of the hill. He looked down to the mouth of the cave. His woman was poking the fire with a twig. Krog sighed deeply. He wished his woman was beautiful, but make-up and hair dyes had not yet been invented. And neither had Immac. Krog picked a handful of red berries and loped down the hill towards the fire and the woman he loved. Language had yet to be invented but he grunted a greeting to his woman and she grunted back. Krog offered her the berries; she snatched them from his hand and crammed them into her black-toothed mouth. 'There should be something called manners,' Krog thought, as he watched the juice from the berries spray from her lips. A dinosaur brayed in the distance; the sound echoed across the Neanderthal landscape. Krog picked up his spear and put his arm protectively around his woman. She turned her face towards him, her lips were stained red. 'My God, you're beautiful,' grunted Krog. His loins stirred. He led his woman into his cave.

Pamela Pigg stayed the night, but intimacy did not take place. At 11 p.m., I suggested that she change her name by Deed Poll. She said it would kill her father. The Piggs went back to the Plantagenets. She said that her only salvation was to change her name by marriage. She looked pointedly at me. I turned away and feigned sleep.

Tuesday, March 13

There was a farmer called Bailey on *Midlands Today*, tonight, claiming that he was forced to feed his live-stock antibiotics and British Airways leftovers, and to keep them in cages in darkness because the public demanded cheap food. Strange, but I do not recall the citizenry rioting outside Parliament for the cause of 5p off a pound of beef. However, I predict that it won't be long before hoteliers, rugby players, jockeys, canoeists, anorak makers, mountaineering boot retailers and mystery tour coach drivers mobilize and march on Downing Street demanding compensation.

Friday, March 16

I went to visit my father today in the isolation ward. He was due to be discharged yesterday, but has contracted yet another hospital superbug. Some of his blood, and several of his mucous membranes, are in the hospital laboratory being tested. Tracy, his barrier nurse, was reading aloud to him an article on foot-and-mouth from the *Daily Telegraph*. When she quoted, 'Farmers are the custodians of the countryside,' my father roared, 'The bastards have ruined the bleeding countryside. They have pulled up the hedges, polluted the rivers, fed their animals on shit, and bled the taxpayer dry.' My father is wildly prejudiced against farmers. In the early days of their marriage, he suspected that my mother had an affair with a maggot farmer. It is strange how such a tenuous connection can colour our opinions. I, myself, have not stepped foot in the county of Kent since my enemy, Barry Kent, had his novel short-listed for the Booker Prize.

I didn't stay long at his bedside, as I was anxious to get back to my prehistoric novel, *Krog From Gork*. I am enjoying the challenge of writing a book set in a time before language was invented. I tried to interest my father in the challenge, but could tell by the way he yawned and closed his eyes that he had little enthusiasm for my latest literary endeavour. After a desultory conversation about the umpiring in Sri Lanka, I left the stifling atmosphere of his isolation cubicle.

Tracy resumed her reading. As I got to the end of the ward, I heard my father shout, 'Nobody compensated me when the electric storage heater industry collapsed. Nobody came to film the rusty heaps of storage heaters lying in the fields.'

Saturday, March 17

My mother has been released from Holloway. The Crown Prosecution Service has lost the papers relating to her case. She was distraught to discover that her newish husband, Ivan Braithwaite, was back living at The Lawns with his ex-wife, Tania. They claim that they are living like brother and sister.

Sunday, March 18, lunchtime

There was a farmer's wife on the midday news sobbing because her healthy baby lambs were going to be slaughtered. Me, William and Glenn watched with tears in our eyes. Then Glenn said, after blowing his nose, 'Dad, what would 'ave 'appened to them little lambs if foot-and-mouth 'adn't broke out?'

I try not to lie to my sons. I replied, 'Those little lambs would have been herded into a truck, driven to a far-away abattoir, killed and hung on a hook, before being cut into pieces.' Perhaps I shouldn't have been so graphic, as both boys have since informed me that, from now on, they will eat only vegetarian food. This is extremely annoying. As I write, a leg of lamb is cooking in the oven.

Monday, March 19

I rang Pandora on her mobile; she was at Wells-next-the-Sea, trying to charm a crowd of suspicious whelk workers. Apparently, female whelks are mutating and growing penises. 'And the bloody cod have practically disappeared,' she complained. I tried to comfort her by saying, 'At least you were not called to give evidence in front of Elizabeth Filkin and her committee in the Vaz case.' Her phone immediately cut off. The signal must be weak on the Norfolk coast.

Tuesday, March 20

Progress on the novel:

Krog squatted behind his wife, picking lice from her matted hair. Her belly was big with child. Krog did not know why. Krog wanted to tell his wife how much he loved her. He wished that somebody would hurry up and invent language and clothes and shampoo. Then Krog spoke to his wife: 'You woman, me man.'

Friday, March 23

Had a FedEx letter from Hamish Mancini in the States. I have not seen him for more than 15 years, though we exchange Christmas cards. He is now living with his alcoholic mother in Idaho.

Hi, Aidy!

Jesus, listen I've got a real big problem and I need advice from you soonest. I got a vacation planned in Great Britain, starting Sunday, April 1. Mom's spiritual advisor, the Rev Moses Hick, told me and Mom that he saw mad cows burning on the runway at Heathrow on the TV news. He tells me that the Old River Thames has flooded Windsor Castle, and that all your British animals, if eaten, will send us mad in 15 years or so. Are things really so bad? I was hoping to visit you and stay a couple of days; travelling with Mom is always an ordeal. She's on two bottles of Jack Daniel's a day now. Please answer soonest.

Hamish Mancini, your ex-pen pal

I replied immediately.

Dear Hamish,

On no account come to England. Heathrow is ringed by army tanks. Dead animals litter the fields. The food in the stores is inedible. We are living on nuts and berries picked from the few surviving hedgerows. Derailed trains have brought our railways to a standstill. Petrol (gas) now costs $20 a gallon, and it is difficult to travel on our motorways. Traffic is gridlocked due to the frequent strip searches conducted by the police as part of their constant search for the foot-and-mouth virus.

Nothing would have given me more pleasure than to have given you and your charming mother board and lodging. However, I strongly advise you NOT to visit this benighted land of mine.

Yours, as ever,

Adrian

P.S. If I were you, I would not think about visiting Britain for at least five years. NOT if you value your life.

I haven't got enough sheets and pillowslips for visitors, and anyway Hamish and his mother speak in exclamation marks. Also, I told him in my last but one Christmas card that I live in a thatched cottage in the countryside. Whereas, tragically, I am living in a social-exclusion zone where there is one tree per thousand people.

Saturday, March 24

William and Glenn have made their mother (not the same woman) a Mother's Day card. Glenn's card showed Sharon sitting on a sofa smoking a fag. Inside, he had written in pseudo gothic script: 'Best wishes on your special day, I love you more than words can say, You're always miserable and sad, That is why I live with Dad.'

William's card showed a black stick woman with 10 fingers on each hand. He had written, with help from me: 'Can I come to live in Africa? All the animals are being shot here, Love from your son, William.'

I bought a card from the garage. It depicted a giraffe with a balloon coming out of its mouth saying, 'I think highly of you Mum.' It was the only one left. The verse inside said: 'Patient, caring, loving, true, I owe my happiness to you'. This was gross hypocrisy on my part. My mother is practically a sociopath and is almost entirely responsible for my malcontent.

Sunday, March 25, Mother's Day

Me and Rosie took our mother to the Holiday Palace Hotel for lunch today. It cost £16.99 a head. Only the lavatories were filthier than the food. Woke in the night, worrying about the pigs' brains I once cooked for John Prescott when I was an offal chef in Soho. Did I sign the poor man's death warrant?

Wrote another paragraph of *Krog From Gork*:

Krog ran his finger down his wife's protruding forehead. He loved her low brow. He hated a woman to be too intellectual.

Saturday, March 31

I'm glad to see the end of this accurs-éd month. William went into the back garden to try out his new red wellingtons. Minutes later, he had to be rescued by me and Glenn after sinking up to his waist in the squelching bog that used to be the lawn.

Michael Fish told me and my fellow British TV gogglers at lunchtime today that the previous 12 months had been the wettest since records had been kept. I said to Michael, 'I'm not surprised, Mike.'

I was about to tell him about William's near miss when I realized, to my horror, that Michael Fish would not have been able to hear me. I must get out more.

As I was cooking the boys' Quorn burgers tonight, I had a sudden brainwave, and phoned Pandora on her direct number at the Ministry of Agriculture, Fisheries and Food. She answered at once. For a joke, I pretended to be the chief vet of Norfolk. I said, 'Moi dear gal, Oi'm the chief vet of Norfolk. Oi'm sorry, gal, but Oi've got bad news. There's been a serious outbreak of beak-and-claw down here. More than 11 million chickens and turkeys are affected.'

She gave an audible gasp. Then said, 'Christ, what next? Is it safe to eat the eggs?'

I answered in my newly acquired Norfolk accent, 'No, my dear, they must be gathered from their coops and stamped, "DO NOT INGEST. THIS EGG IS CARRYING THE BEAK AND CLAW VIRUS".'

There was silence and she stifled a sob. She then shouted across the office, 'Get me Tony, at once!' She then spoke urgently to somebody nearby, and I heard a male voice shout, 'Fuckin' 'ell, there's beak-'n'-claw in Norfolk!' He sounded hysterical.

I was starting to regret my deception, but when Pandora asked me if she should arrange for the poultry to be slaughtered and the eggs to be buried, for some reason I answered, 'Put the birds out of their misery, by all means, but the eggs could come in useful – for throwing at politicians during the run-up to the general election.'

After I'd slammed down the phone, I was ashamed of myself. Pandora was so proud of her recent promotion to junior minister for poultry. I tried to ring back, but the phones in her office were permanently engaged. What I had intended to suggest to her was that, rather than destroy infected sheep, instead each

household in Britain be given a skinned and disem-
bowelled carcass to put in the freezer. After all, foot-
and-mouth presents no danger to we homo sapiens.
(To keep things fair, vegetarians could be given a
token for a bag of turnips or something.) This would
surely win votes for New Labour.

Sunday, April 1, April Fool's Day

A Leicester courier firm, 24–7, woke me early this
morning with the most wonderful letter of my life:

Dear Adrian Mole,
   My name is Louise Moore. I am an editor at Penguin
Books Ltd. I will cut quickly to the chase. While
lunching in the Ivy yesterday with Will Self and Martin
Amis, I could not help but overhear a conversation at
the next table between two agents. They were discussing
your unfinished manuscript, *Krog From Gork*. I was
gripped by the story of how Krog invents man's first
language, thus enabling him to tell his wife that he loves
her.
   Penguin would like to offer you £1 million for a
two-book deal. Please ring me at 9.30 a.m. on Monday.
   Yours sincerely,
   Louise Moore

Monday, April 2

My birthday cards were illustrated by the usual symbols of masculinity: vintage cars, foaming tankards and fishing rods.

At 9.30 precisely, I rang Ms Moore's number. Pandora answered. 'April Fool, you birthday boy bastard,' she shouted before slamming down the phone.

Friday, April 6
Arthur Askey Way, Ashby de la Zouch

A belated birthday card from Pamela Pigg. On the front, a picture of a middle-aged git, sitting at a rustic table outside a thatched pub. A black labrador lies at the git's feet, next to a wicker basket from which protrude several fishing rods, nets, etc. The git is wearing a green waxed jacket and a deerstalker, and is raising a foaming tankard to his self-satisfied lips. In the background is a vintage car, presumably owned by the git.

For how long did Pamela shop for this card? And when she found it, did she exclaim, 'At last! This is the perfect card for Adrian Mole'? She must know by now that I hate thatch, dogs, tankards, fishing, tweed

– in fact, almost everything to do with the countryside. I am urbane to my very fingertips. Inside, Pamela had written: 'Adrian, Mon Amour, let's try again. Sex is not everything, Love Piglet'.

Query: do I want to try again with Pamela? Most of our trysts seem to end in tears, snot and recriminations. She is ludicrously oversensitive: last autumn, when we were walking in the woods, she wept because the leaves were leaving 'their mothers' (the trees).

Saturday, April 7

Against my better judgement, I rang Pamela and asked her to accompany me to Nigel's official coming-out party. I could not risk being mistaken for a single gay man. I regretted my invitation as soon as I saw her outfit. No woman over 17 should wear a sequinned boob tube, in my opinion. And her comedy earrings were not at all amusing. Nigel's parents looked shell-shocked – his mother still thinks his homosexuality is a 'silly phrase [sic] he is going through'.

That night, after yet another failed attempt at sexual congress (her fault, not mine), Pamela turned her back on me and began to weep piteously. I longed for sleep, but felt compelled to offer her comfort. Unfortunately, she was still there in the morning, naked, apart from the comedy earrings. When William barged into my bedroom, he said, disapprovingly, 'You will have to get married now, Dad.' He has never seen me in bed with a woman before, not even his mother.

Sunday, April 8

Pamela suggested that we go out for lunch *en famille*. She recommended Ye Olde Carvery in Frisby-On-The-Wreake. Glenn and William were excited – they rarely eat out. On the way, in the car, I explained that Frisby-On-The-Wreake was a notorious centre for paganism. Pamela contradicted me violently, saying that Frisby had won best-kept hanging basket prize for three years running. I pointed out that the two could easily co-exist, and Glenn said diplomatically, 'Yeah, a witch can 'ave 'an 'anging basket.'

Ye Olde Carvery was full of wax-jacketed gits talking in loud voices about the poor cow who'd put her foot in it. I assumed they were banging on about foot and mouth, but Pamela had picked up a copy of the *Mail on Sunday* and told me the Countess of Wessex had been entrapped by a reporter dressed as an Arab sheikh into calling John Major 'wooden', William Hague 'a puppet', and foxes 'vermin'.

The carvery did not cater for vegetarians. Indeed, a glance at the trays of ye olde foode congealing behind the bar told me that Ye Olde Carvery did not cater for any person with a normal appetite, tastebuds, etc. On the way out, one of the gits laughed at Pamela's comedy earrings. I could hardly object.

Wednesday, April 11

Awake all night with irritating dry cough. Sweated profusely.

Thursday, April 12

TB has broken out only two kilometres from my door! And I have all the symptoms. Dr Ng was summoned. He angrily removed a red sequin from the back of my throat.

Friday, April 13, Good Friday

Why do banks close on bank holidays? They should be open when so many are free to use them. I wished to query a statement saying I had spent £104.49 on Belgian chocolates at a shop in Lewes, so rang a call centre in Southend. I told a youth called Gary that I never bought chocolate due to the effect it has on my skin, and had never been to Lewes.

He said: 'Perhaps it was an internet transaction.'

I repeated testily that I could not tolerate chocolate.

He said. 'Perhaps you bought it for someone else – it is Easter.'

I said angrily. 'I am a poor man: £104.49 exceeds my weekly income.'

He snapped, 'The standing order to your news-agent could keep an African village in food for a month.'

At this moment, Glenn shouted from the toilet that there was no paper. I put Gary on hold. When I came back, 'Greensleeves' was playing, so I went to my bank, only to find the doors locked.

Glenn was miserable all day. He asked if he could paint his bedroom black. When I asked what was wrong he said. 'Why do they call it Good Friday? It weren't for poor Jesus, were it?' He explained that he had trodden on a drawing pin this morning: 'It brung it 'ome to me what it must 'ave been like on the cross, Dad.' He then asked if he could have a Heroes Easter egg. William's egg of choice is Barbie. Worrying.

Saturday, April 14

Had an email from Hamish Mancini: 'Yo, Adi, I'm FedExing a 100lb bag of Idaho's finest potatoes, because you don't got none in England cos of the floods and plagues. We are praying for you and your family.'

Sunday, April 15, Easter Day

Pamela came round with an egg-decorating kit.

William's eggs were a riot of primary colours: Glenn's depicted Jesus on the cross. He wrote a bubble out of Jesus's mouth. 'Father, why hast thou forsaken me?', which disturbed Pamela: 'For God's sake, Glenn, lighten up. It's Easter!' Later, while William played with the packing of his Barbie egg and Glenn watched *The Greatest Story Ever Told*, she led me to my room and gave me an erotic Easter egg, the centre of which contained a pair of edible knickers. She was keen for me to break it open and retrieve them. I was less keen: a glance at the ingredients told me they were chock-a-block with obscure chemicals and multi-syllable flavourings.

Sunday, April 22
Ashby de la Zouch

Last Sunday, I forced the boys to sit and listen to *Go4it*, the new Radio 4 children's programme. I was annoyed when, after only five minutes, Glenn complained, 'It's for posh kids, innit?' William fell asleep during the Sir Steve Redgrave interview. I woke him and said, 'Sir Steve has won five gold medals for this country. The least you can do is stay awake while he's talking.'

This evening, we again sat down to listen. I was enthralled by the interview with Thunderbirds creator Gerry Anderson. I was once besotted with Lady Penelope. She was the subject of my first sexual fantasy. I still like women who are a bit on the wooden side. Pandora Braithwaite MP, the love of my life, has a carved look about her. Though it is the Labour Party who are now pulling her strings. Ha ha!

She was on the news tonight, wearing Prada wellingtons and a tweed suit, trying to assure angry country folk why a massive hole containing hundreds of thousands of noxious, decomposing cows and sheep would not become a health hazard. A reporter shouted, 'Have you signed the compact, Pandora?' She snapped, 'The only compact I have any use for has the name Chanel embossed on the lid.'

Monday, April 23

Pandora's remark has landed her in trouble with the CRE. She's been ordered to have her photo taken with a black or brown person. She rang to ask if William was available. I said, 'The child's skin is not for hire.' She asked me for Mohammed's mobile number and then rang off.

Tuesday, April 24

When I went to the BP garage for a box of Coco Pops, Mohammed was bursting with the news that Pandora had rung him and had invited herself and a *Newsnight* crew to dinner last night. She had requested chicken tikka masala. Mohammed said, 'Me missus were a bit put out, cos she usually gets fish and chips on Tuesdays, but you can't deny Pandora owt when she orders you about in that posh voice, can you?' He asked me what side *Newsnight* was on.

Naturellement, I viewed the programme with great interest. Pandora was wearing her Alexander McQueen-designed Punjabi suit she'd last worn to the inaugural meeting of Ashby's Anglo-Asian women's rugby team.

Went to bed and listened to a radio phone-in. Most of the callers were ringing in to talk about Phoenix the calf who is healthy but has a death sentence hanging over him. He is due to be executed by a ministry vet tomorrow.

Thursday, April 26
Ashby de la Zouch, 10.30 p.m.

Thank God Phoenix has been reprieved. William cried himself to sleep last night, and Glenn spoke darkly about travelling to Membury in Devon and joining the junior wing of a militant vegetarian splinter group called Sprouts, who were planning to resist evil MAFF, the calf murderers. His motives were not entirely altruistic. He has been bewitched by Joanna

Lumley since seeing her pleading so eloquently for the calf's life on TV. This is worrying: Ms Lumley is enchanting, but she is old enough to be his grandmother.

Saturday, April 28

I went to the garage for milk early this morning, and was alarmed to find Mohammed being given oxygen by two paramedics. He had been overcome by the fumes emanating from a pile of the restyled *Guardian Weekend* magazines. I stayed until he had recovered enough to gasp, 'This allergy could be the end of my career as a forecourt newsagent, Moley.'

This afternoon, William ran home from the grotty recreation ground in tears, after a big white kid called him a 'mongrel'. I reminded him that he had in his veins the blood of a Nigerian aristocrat, a Norfolk potato farmer, a Scottish engine driver, a Welsh witch and that, by virtue of being born in this country, and as defined by the OED, he was as English as Prince Philip. The kid refused to be comforted, until he was invited by Glenn to watch a video of Joanna Lumley in her role as Purdey in *The New Avengers*.

Sunday, April 29

Filling in the census form took longer than expected. I agonized over the work-related questions. Eventually, I ticked the 'Yes' box, and admitted that I had worked for three hours on my novel, *Krog From Gork*.

William didn't seem to belong to any ethnic group. I rang the helpline and spoke to a bloke called Len Cook. He seemed irritated by my explanation of William's various bloodlines. In the end, I settled for box B – Mixed other, and wrote British/Black African.

Glenn hovered over the religious question, but eventually declared himself to be a Buddhist after I had given him a breakdown of the world's other great religions. He liked the fact that Buddhists shaved their heads and were careful not to tread on ants.

Saturday, May 5

Dear Prime Minister,

I have just watched your foreign secretary, Robin Cook, on the TV news. However, I have no idea what the man was talking about since I could not understand a word he said. Surely it is time he was given an official translator. Failing this, perhaps subtitles could be used.

I am a keen follower of foreign affairs, and resent being disenfranchised by Mr Cook's incoherent babble. Incidentally, I like the new spectacles – they give you gravitas, something you have been lacking lately due to your own casual articulation.

I remain, sir,

A. A. Mole

An official called Colin Dodge telephoned from customs and excise at Heathrow airport this afternoon. He informed me (rather curtly, I thought) that the Idaho potatoes sent as emergency food by Hamish Mancini had been confiscated under the anti-Colorado-beetle restrictions. I emailed Hamish and warned him against sending any more food parcels, and told him that the foot-and-mouth crisis was now under control and that food was now available in the shops.

Hamish emailed back: 'I seen the weekly news round-up today, oh boy! There was crowds of crazy reds an' anarchists rioting in London town. When's it gonna be safe for me and Mom to visit? I wanna vacation in that cute thatched cottage you live in.'

Monday, May 7, bank holiday

Vince Ludlow, my neighbour, threw a 'Welcome Home Ronnie' party today. He has never met Biggs, but obviously feels an affinity with the train robber. All day, and long into the night, our street was clogged with criminal traffic. A rumour circulated that Mad Frankie Fraser was sitting on the Ludlows' settee, eating crab paste sandwiches. The noise was intolerable. But I decided not to complain, as I did not wish my feet to be sawn off at the ankles. Instead, I took Glenn and William for a ramble in the countryside.

On the outskirts of Little Snickerton, I parked in a lay-by and tried to get the boys to leave the car, but neither of them would budge. They are both under the impression that the countryside is ruled by despotic farmers who hate city dwellers. Eventually, I turned the car round and drove back.

Friday, May 25

I visited my father in his isolation cubicle today. I couldn't be bothered to go through the showering, putting on sterile gown, mask and boots rigmarole, so I was gesticulating to him through the observation panel in the door. I was just about to give him the thumbs up before leaving for home, when his consultant, Mr R. T. Train, approached, trailed by a gang of medical students. I moved aside and was present throughout Train's lesson in diagnostic technique. He pointed through the glass to my father, who was sitting up in bed reading a laminated, germ-free copy of the *Daily Express*.

'Take good notice of that patient,' drawled Train. 'He is recovering from repeated hospital infections, but he is also suffering from an interesting psychological condition. Can anyone guess its nature?' A small Chinese youth said, 'Does he think that the *Daily Express* is a newspaper, sir?'

When the laughter had died down, Train said indulgently, 'Well done, Wang. Anyone else?' The students took it in turns to peer at my father.

Eventually a black woman – who reminded me a little of my ex-wife Jo-Jo – said, 'There are three portraits of William Hague in the room. Is he an obsessive?' Train said, 'Well observed.' He then spoke to the fat Englishman in the group. 'Read the patient's notes and give me your diagnosis, Dr Worthington.' Worthington's fat face creased in concentration. He read through my father's notes.

Eventually he looked up and said, 'The poor sod's

delusional. He thinks Hague is going to be the next prime minister.'

A defeated-looking woman cleaner approached with a bucket of filthy water and a rancid mop. She was wearing a cheap nylon overall, emblazoned with the logo Priva Clean. She tried to go into my father's room before being stopped by Train, who ordered her to change the water in the bucket, and don sterile clothes. She whined, 'I ain't got time. I gotta clean three more wards and an operatin' theatre before I knock off.'

Saturday, May 26

Pandora has abandoned the electorate of Ashby de la Zouch and gone to Hay-on-Wye to seek a private audience with ex-president Clinton. She packed what she called a Lewinsky frock. She clearly has no morals whatsoever.

Saturday, June 2
Ashby de la Zouch

Glenn woke me early with the alarming news that Prince Charles had gone mad with a Kalashnikov and killed his entire family, 'cos of Camilla'. I switched on Five Live and was reassured that the massacre had taken place in Kathmandu, and that (presumably) our own royals were safe and reasonably well.

Sunday, June 3

Pandora knocked on my door as I was washing up this morning. She placed a hand on my cheek and purred, 'Can I count on your vote, as usual, sweetie?' I coldly informed her that I had become disillusioned due to her habit of breaking promises and that I intended to vote for the Socialist Alliance candidate, Abbo Palmer. She left her canvassers on the rain-lashed street and pushed her way into my kitchen, snarling, 'What broken promises?'

I counted out the disappointments on my fingers. I was still wearing my yellow Marigolds at the time, so the effect may not have been as dramatic as I had intended. When I got to the last rubber digit I said, 'Finally, Pandora, you promised to marry me as soon as we were 16 years of age and could afford the train fare to Gretna Green.' I took out my wallet and pro-duced the written evidence: a note she had scribbled in a double geography lesson more than 20 years ago.

The sight of her childish, loopy handwriting almost brought tears to my eyes.

Pandora scanned the note, then turned it over. On the back was a graph showing the decline of Britain's manufacturing base under Thatcher. She murmured, 'Interesting,' then asked if she could have the note, as it meant so much to her. I replied, 'Certainly not, I have kept this love note in my wallet, close to my heart, for two decades. It reminds me of the time when we were 15 and rapturously in love.'

We were interrupted when a woman canvasser, in need of Immac for the upper lip and chin, knocked on the door and said, 'The *Newsnight* camper van has just crashed into your car, Pandora. Jeremy Vine wants your insurance details.'

Midnight
Pandora has just been interviewed on *Newsnight*, by an unusually deferential Jeremy Vine. The set consisted of the blown-up note. (On the graph side.)

Friday, June 8
Ashby de la Zouch

I woke at 9.30 to find myself on the sofa. The television was showing Ffion's sad but brave face. Glenn was sitting on the floor slopping cornflakes on to the new Ikea rug. With his mouth full, he said, 'Tory boy's doin' a runner, Dad.' There was the smell of burnt toast, William came in with a plateful of buttered cinders, half of which fell on to the rug. I was too exhausted to shout and sank back on to the new Ikea tapestry cushions. I do not function well on two hours' sleep.

When I next woke, Tony and Cherie were in a small British car being driven to the palace. Glenn and William were still in their pyjamas eating fruit cocktail and the Häagen-Dazs ice cream that I keep for Sunday teatime use only. I croaked to Glenn, 'Did Pandora get in?' A tiny cube of pineapple and a dribble of juice fell from the teaspoon he was wielding like a garden spade.

The rug now resembled a small municipal tip, the ethnic pattern could hardly be seen. Glenn swallowed, and, sounding alarmingly like Peter Snow, gabbled, 'Yes, Dad, she got in with 23, 431 votes, a majority of

8,157, tha's 52.06% of the vote, but she's down a bit cos there were a swing to the Tories of 3.64%. An' there was a 65.79% turnout, tha's a lot 'igher than the national average.'

I was impressed with the boy's grasp of statistics. I may steer him towards a degree in mathematics. William brought me a cup of tepid tea and placed it on the rug. Thirty seconds later, the cup lay on its side, having been toppled by Glenn demonstrating a kick-boxing move.

Midday

I ordered the boys to get dressed for school. When I next woke it was four o'clock and the school day had ended. Glenn said, 'My 'ead of year rang, Dad, he wanted to know why I ain't been to school. So I told 'im I 'ad to stay at 'ome to look after you, cos you wunt get off the settee.'

I snapped back. 'Couldn't you have invented a stomach upset or something?'

Glenn said, 'I jus' told the truth, Dad. Were I wrong?'

Since I'd been ranting about the dishonesty of politicians throughout the election campaign I didn't know how to answer the boy, so I feigned sleep.

Thursday, June 14

Glenn asked what I do for a living today. I told him I was a writer. 'I never see you do no writin',' he said accusingly. I told him that I am an unpublished writer, and explained that there was a conspiracy in the publishing industry to keep me out. He took the manuscript of my latest novel, *Krog From Gork*, to read in bed. I am enormously pleased that he is taking such an interest in my literary life.

Pamela Pigg has taken my advice and is going out with Alan Clarke, the amateur folk singer. She rang to tell me that their first date went 'splendidly'. He took her to The Friends tandoori restaurant. She said that Pandora was dining at an adjacent table with some metropolitans who were opining that Ann Widdecombe is the result of an experiment at Porton Down. Apparently, she escaped before the trials could be concluded. This explains a lot.

Friday, June 15

I asked Glenn what he thought of *Krog From Gork*. He looked shifty and mumbled, 'I ain't got past the third page yet.' I asked him what he thought of the three he had read. Glenn stroked his new Mohican haircut and said, 'Nothin' 'appens, Dad.'

I snapped, 'Of course nothing happens. I'm writing about a prehistoric man who suffers from ennui. What do you expect him to do all day? Send text messages to his fellow primitives?'

At 11.30 a.m., Glenn returned from school with a note:

Dear Parent/Guardian/Principal Carer,

Glenn arrived at school this morning with a most alarming haircut. Within minutes of entering the playground he was surrounded by a large circle of 'admirers'. Several of the first-year boys were literally sick with excitement. The school rules state unequivocally that 'students' hair must not be subject to the vagaries of fashion'. Glenn is hereby excluded until his hair can be described in these terms.

From now, I'll teach the boy at home.

Saturday, June 16

Watched the Trooping of the Colour with the boys. I was filled with pride. Is there another country on earth whose soldiers would march through torrents of water without complaint?

I was annoyed to overhear Glenn say to William, 'The monarchy's finished, Willy. They ain't got the sense to come in out the rain.'

Sunday, June 24

I had a minor breakdown in the vinegar aisle of the supermarket this morning. I was completely unable to choose between the 64 vinegars on offer. I walked up and down in an agony of indecision. Glenn said, 'Dad, we've bin 'ere 20 minutes. What's up?' I didn't trust myself to speak, for fear that the tears gathering in my eyes would be released. Eventually, Glenn grabbed a bottle at random and threw it into the trolley. I saw that it was lemongrass flavour and tried to replace it on the shelf, but Glenn prevented me and we moved on to the oil aisle, where once again I was confronted with a horrific choice. They stretched into the distance: grapeseed, extra-virgin olive, sesame seed, sunflower, Crisp 'n' Dry, basil, stir-fry ... As I was hovering between them, an announcement came over the in-store Tannoy – a woman who sounded as though she had a small grapefruit stuck in her mouth intoned: 'Would Mr

Mole return to the crèche immediately. Mr Mole, return to the crèche.'

I left Glenn with the trolley and rushed off, lurid images of crèche-type accidents filling my mind: had William been suffocated by the myriad coloured balls that filled the toddlers' jumping pit? Had he stabbed a paintbrush in his eye? Was he lying unconscious at the foot of the toddlers' jungle gym? If so, I would pursue the supermarket through the courts and force them into paying record amounts of compensation. Nothing less than £30 million could possibly compensate me for an injury done to my precious child.

The supervisor, whose badge told me she was Mary-Lou Hattersley, was waiting for me with a tearful William. Ms Hattersley (6 out of 10: large breasts, clear skin, blonde hair, but needs a good cut, legs hidden by trousers) said, 'He wants his mummy.' I was astonished to hear this. William never mentions his mother. I explained that my ex-wife lived in Nigeria. She flicked her hair back and murmured, 'Have you remarried, Mr Mole?'

I assured her that I was single, then, by way of conversation, asked her if she was related to Lord Hattersley, the hothead revolutionary. 'Incontrovertibly,' she said.

I am in love. Glenn's shopping came to £185.99.

Saturday, June 30

I am still in love with the supervisor of Safeway's in-store crèche, Mary-Lou Hattersley. She has the widest vocabulary of any woman I have ever known – and that includes Pandora, who lectured in semantics at Oxford for a while.

Mary-Lou, or ML as she likes to be called, claims that both she and Roy Hattersley, her very distant relation, have inherited the same genes from Isaiah Hattersley, 'an autodidact night soil man'. He was a follower of 'disestablishmentarianism', she told me as she pinned William's name-badge on his new *Shrek* T-shirt.

Instead of doing a weekly shop, I now find myself visiting the store daily. William is complaining that he is fed up with the crèche, but I have bribed him with the promise of a trip to McDonald's. Yes, I have sunk that low! But I am a prisoner of love. I have to see her dirty blonde hair. Those fiery, intelligent eyes. She wore a skirt yesterday, so I was able to assess her legs. They are not bad, though when we are better acquainted I will advise her to avoid shorts and mini-skirts.

Monday, July 2

Glenn asked if he could have the day off school to watch Henman get beaten. For some reason he hates him; he can't explain why.

On no account must I tell ML how I feel about her. I have made that mistake before. In my experience, women don't like protestations of love from strangers. They fail to return calls, ignore messages and sometimes get their brothers to throw you off the doorstep.

My father has been discharged from hospital with a clean bill of health. However, he has been told by his doctors that he must rest at home and take things easy for a few months.

My mother rang me at midnight from Majorca to tell me that my father spent the night in the police station in Palma. He had a fight in the taxi queue at the airport. Apparently, he was maddened by thirst and the heat, and when a French family pushed in front of him he cracked and screamed, 'Oi, Frogface! Hop off!' The Frenchman said something about foot-and-mouth, and my father went berserk and kicked the man's luggage into the gutter.

It came as a complete shock to me that my mother

and my father have gone on holiday with each other. Have their spouses given their permissions?

Tuesday, July 3

Glenn has been very subdued lately, he has stopped talking and is off his food. I tried to talk to him, but he brushed me off as though I were a loathsome insect.

I consulted the handbook *Parents Are From Hove, Teenagers Are From Brighton*. On page 31 it said, 'Keep the channels of communication open, but do not let your teen control the domestic agenda. If your questions are ignored, smile and say, "I hear your silence. Should you wish to share your thoughts with me, I will always be here for you, 24–7."'

William has put his small foot down and has refused to be deposited into Safeway's crèche twice a day at 8 a.m. and 4 p.m. This means that I no longer have a valid excuse to see Mary-Lou Hattersley, the divine supervisor of that kiddies' establishment. I will have to borrow a toddler. I have to see her.

Prince Philip and Prince Charles were on the news, stamping about in knee-high boots and wearing cocked hats, medals and epaulettes; they looked like extras from *Zulu*. Don't they know the game is up? It is ridiculous in the age of interactive television. In fact, I may write to the privy council and suggest that in future the royals withdraw from public life and satisfy the lust of their monarchist followers by appearing in a *Big Brother*-like TV show. They could then dress up and swagger around in as many costumes as they liked. It would certainly cut down on their transport costs, which I understand are considerable.

Wednesday, July 4, American Independence Day

Glenn is being bullied at school. He is the only boy in his class who does not have his own mobile phone. He is a pariah.

Bumped into Pamela Pigg in Safeway. She is still going out with Alan Clarke. He was wearing an Aran sweater. It is chilly by the frozen-food cabinets, but I was comfortable enough in my shirtsleeves, so perhaps he was going on to a 'gig' after shopping. I suppose there must be a few folk clubs left in the land.

*

Mr Blair was said to have been 'savaged' by his own backbenchers at prime minister's questions. This was a gross distortion. He was asked a few facetious questions by a trio of toothless curs.

Monday, July 16
Ashby de la Zouch

This morning I borrowed a toddler from the Ludlows next door and took it to Safeway's crèche, which is supervised by the most erotically intelligent woman alive on the planet Earth, Mary-Lou Hattersley. It is my only means of seeing her, and William refuses to cooperate, the ungrateful little swine.

The toddler was very quiet in the back of the car. I wasn't surprised – the Ludlows don't believe in talking to their children. As Mrs Ludlow told me once: 'It only encourages 'em to prattle on an' ask stupid bleedin' questions.' Secretly, I have some sympathy with this child-rearing theory. I have often been tormented by William's constant demands to know 'how', 'when' and 'why'. Only yesterday, as we watched the riots on *Sky News*, he asked me why it was 'always men and boys fighting and never the ladies and girls'. I told him that females have a subtler method of conducting warfare, but this led to a further raft of questions, which stopped only when I pretended to fall asleep on top of the washing machine.

As we drove to Safeway, I realized I had no idea what the toddler was called or even what its sex was. It was wearing earrings and had an unpleasant scowling expression on its face. I took a guess and registered the child as Emily Ludlow, aged two-and-a-half years. After 'Emily' had been divested of its shoes and was being led into the play area by a crèche minion, I engaged Mary-Lou in conversation. Knowing her interest in politics, I asked her opinion on the Tory leadership race. She scoffed, 'I'm more intellectually challenged by wondering who will be up for eviction in the Big Brother house.' We are both agreed that Paul and Helen's burgeoning romance is horrible but compulsive viewing. It is like watching two very stupid white rhinos attempting to mate – one is repelled by the sight, but touched that two such rare creatures have found each other.

I tore myself away from her to grab a tin of Heinz Organic Baked Beans 'n' Sausages. When I returned, Mary-Lou was stern-faced and 'Emily' was wearing a pair of the crèche's emergency mini Y-fronts. I am banned from using the crèche for life.

Thursday, July 19
Ashby de la Zouch

I attended William's school sports day today. The school field was sold off to Nolite Warehouse Ltd in February, so the races took place in a roped-off section of its new car park. I was just about to climb into my dustbin liner bag for the single parents' sack race, when the headmaster announced over the Tannoy that the jury had returned and that Jeffrey Archer had been sent to jail for four years. Spontaneous cheering broke out from the assembled company, the workmen on the scaffolding of the windowless warehouse broke into song with 'You'll Never Walk Alone', passing cars sounded their hooters and a light aircraft flying overhead did a figure-of-eight in the summer sky. The headmaster announced that there would be a five-minute delay for competitors to compose themselves.

Archer has succeeded in bringing the country together in joy. After Henman, the Lions and England's dropped catches, we needed a glorious victory.

I came last. William would not look me in the eye when I finally passed the finish line. The winner was Trixie Woodhead, who I know for a fact is drawing disability living allowance.

Saturday, July 21

My parents have been to see me to give me an 'update' on what my mother called 'the ongoing situation regarding our marriage'. They held hands across the kitchen table and my father said sheepishly, 'We can't live with each other, but we can't live without each other, son.'

William, who had been listening, said with the brutal candour of the child, 'You'll both have to die, then.'

I advised them to try self-discipline. (They are both still married to other people, namely Pandora's parents.) My father whined, 'We were both teenagers in the '60s, so haven't got any self-discipline.' As they were leaving, I told my mother that blue jeans should never be worn with creases, or wrinkles.

Monday, July 23, 1 p.m.

Pandora has invited me to a 'shepherd's pie and Krug party' this evening. It is not clear what we will be celebrating.

Midnight

Nobody told me that Pandora's guests were meant to wear Mary and Jeffrey fancy dress. Personally, I found the sight of so many Mary Archer lookalikes slightly disturbing. I like a bit of animation in my women.

Friday, July 27

I allowed William to stay up late to watch the climax of *Big Brother*. I think it is important that small children be allowed to participate in events of national importance. My mother and father came round to join us, bringing two large bags of curry-flavoured Twiglets and a bottle of Raspberry Stolichnaya. My mother grew increasingly hysterical after Dean was evicted from the house, leaving Helen and Brian. She passionately wanted Helen to win, saying, 'Why should the intelligent people win all the glittering prizes? It's time a stupid person won something for a change.'

My father said, 'I don't mind her being thick, it's her great big gob I object to.' I feigned indifference, but secretly I had my fingers crossed for Brian. I slipped into the kitchen and was dialling my vote in when Glenn caught me at it. I had to pretend to be phoning Dial-A-Pizza, so Brian's vote cost me £32.59.

As we watched Helen squealing like a tortured piglet over Paul Clarke's present of a Gucci handbag and shoes, William asked, 'Will Helen and Paul Clarke be having sexual intercourse tonight, Dad?'

My father shouted, 'Go and wash your mouth out, you dirty-minded sod.'

But, as Glenn said, 'He's only sayin' what everbody's thinkin', Grandad.'

I lay awake, pondering yet again on the true nature of my sexuality. Did I vote for Brian out of gay solidarity or because he is a semi-erudite Irish eccentric? I garnered the evidence: a) I like Kylie Minogue; b) I sleep with a lavender pillow; c) I am no good at sex with women; d) I am very fussy about my sheets, pillowcases and towels.

Saturday, July 28

Heatwave. I went to Pandora's surgery this morning. It was the only way to see her, since she does not reply to my emails, or return my frequent phone calls or text messages. She was most unsuitably dressed for an MP. I know it is hot, but her outfit of cropped top and micro-shorts lacked gravitas. I had wanted to ask her about the euro, but I could not concentrate because of the sweat trickling between her tanned, pointy breasts. So we ended up talking about *Big Brother*. She is intimate with Michael Jackson at Channel 4, and suggested I put myself forward as a *BB* candidate in 2002.

Saturday, August 4
Ashby de la Zouch

William, the ardent monarchist, made a birthday card for the Queen Mother this morning using scraps of card and paper taken from the recycling bag. He had fashioned her hat from milk bottle tops – she looked as if she was wearing a Darth Vader helmet.

I, for one, do not believe the old woman was given a blood transfusion on Thursday. I think she is kept going by a secret serum that is not yet available to us common people (or Princess Margaret). I read somewhere that axolotls can constantly regenerate themselves, thus living for ever. Is it my imagination or does the Queen Mother look a teensy bit lizard-like lately? Will she be the first 200-year-old woman?

Sunday, August 5

I am no financial expert, but I feel in my bones that
we will be living under the jackboot of recession by
Christmas. I decided to forgo the interest on my
Alliance & Leicester 30-Day Notice Deposit Account,
and withdrew the entire amount, £619.07. I took
Glenn and William to Safeway and bought a frozen
turkey, a Christmas pudding, three packets of Mr
Kipling's mince pies, a bag of frozen sprouts and a
box of sage and onion stuffing. I also took advantage
of the various in-store two-for-the-price-of-one
offers, but was disgusted that Safeway is not yet selling
Christmas crackers.

Once the Christmas food shopping was complete,
I treated the boys to lunch in the Safeway cafeteria.
Pamela Pigg and Alan Clarke were in there,
canoodling over their All-Day Breakfasts. Pamela told
me that she had bumped into Nigel and his new
partner, Peter Painter, in the Sea Shanty Folk Club
last night.

Alan stroked his beard and drawled, 'Yeah, we all got
on like a house on fire, they're coming to our fondue
party tomorrow night. Why don't you join us?'

Pamela gushed, 'Alan is going to sing for us after
dinner. He has recently unearthed some haymaking

songs written by Isaiah Blackhead, from Stowmarket.'

'I'm doing an OU course on "the music of the idiot savant",' he said. Then, to my horror, he began to sing: 'Lay in the hay, my comely gal, And take my sickle in youse hand.' Glenn blushed fiercely and fled. I followed with William.

Tuesday, August 7
Ashby de la Zouch

The fondue party was held at Alan Clarke's thatched cottage in Mangold Parva. According to local gossip, Mangold Parva is a hotbed of dogging in the car park behind the mini supermarket. It is also rumoured to be the headquarters of the East Midlands black magic circles. In 1974, several donkeys mysteriously disappeared overnight and were believed to have been ritually sacrificed. Alan Clarke fancies himself as a local historian. As we twirled our fondue forks over the pan of bubbling cheese, he regaled his guests with anecdotes about his life in the village. The guests were Pamela Pigg, me, Glenn, Nigel and Peter Painter.

I took Glenn with me because it is time the boy was taught how to conduct himself in sophisticated company. Before we got out of the car, I warned him not to say serviette, or to inform the other guests that his ambition is to be a heterosexual when he grows up.

To a background of Bob Dylan's harmonica, we chomped through seven varieties of hot cheese. I incautiously mentioned how saddened I had been to hear of the death of Larry Adler and added that, in my opinion, Adler had been the greatest harmonica player the world had ever known. Peter Painter said camply, 'I wouldn't slash my wrists if I never heard the harmonica again.' Alan jabbed his fondue fork angrily into the rough-hewn table, stormed over to the stereo and removed the long-player from the turntable.

There was an awkward silence, which Glenn broke eventually by saying, 'When I grow up, I want to be a heterosexual.'

I was glad to get out of that cottage and rejoin the 21st century – personally, I think Alan Clarke knows what happened to those donkeys.

Friday, August 10

A bombshell! I was idly turning the pages of the *Ashby Bugle* tonight, when I saw the headline 'Third Time Lucky For Ashby Couple?' On the right-hand side was a photograph of my parents' wedding day, taken in the late 1960s. Underneath was another photograph of my parents' wedding day, taken in the late 1980s. I read to my horror that they were intending to marry again, for the third time. I immediately rang my mother. She said, 'We were going to tell you. Some bastard at the *Ashby Bugle* has leaked the story.'

Saturday, August 18

Today, I was a guest at my parents' third wedding. I was a four-month-old foetus when my mother first married my father. I, of course, remember nothing of the occasion – though my dear, dead grandma, May Mole, told me that my mother disgraced herself at the reception by accidentally setting fire to her wedding veil while attempting to light a Capstan with a broken Swan Vesta match.

My father put the blaze out with a bowl of cling peaches in juice, snatched from the buffet. In the resulting confusion, Grandma's 75 home-stuffed vol-au-vents (one per guest) were despoiled. Although only a foetus, I feel sure that this unsavoury incident made me into a non-smoker, with an aversion to swans.

Today's ceremony was conducted at County Hall,

the administrative nerve centre of Leicestershire. It was somewhat disconcerting to look up from the baggy faces of my lovelorn parents pledging their vows, to see a County Hall *apparatchik* photocopying what appeared to be fixed-penalty notices in an adjacent office. If I ever marry again, I will make sure that the setting is suitably romantic. Rutland Water at sunset is said to be a breathtaking sight, though in the summer midges might present a problem.

The reception took place in the One-Stop Centre function room on a nearby council estate. As we guests queued up to offer our congratulations to the bride and groom, we were forced to rub shoulders with benefits claimants, young offenders and a pensioners' ping-pong group. I'm the most liberal and democratic of men, but surely a hotel would have been more suitable?

The musical entertainment was provided by Alan Clarke and his folk group, The Shanty Men, who wore matching Aran sweaters and sang about herrings. I was glad when one of them, Abbo Palmer, broke off and announced that Clarke was 50 that day. Clarke looked horror-struck and Pamela Pigg, his present amour, said to me, 'The bloody liar, he told me he was 37 and a half.'

My father stood up and made a speech about the 'happiest day of his life' – his voice was blurry with sentimental tears. Unfortunately he was talking about something Ian Botham did 20 years ago at Headingley.

Saturday, August 25

I fear I am losing the battle to mould William's character to my own satisfaction. He does not seem to appreciate high culture and has appalling taste in music and literature. He's only an infant, but at his age Mozart was selling out concerts all over Europe. I played the whole of Wagner's 'Ring Cycle' on my stereo this week, hoping that constant exposure to the shrieking and wailing would break down his defences. It failed. As the last note faded, William rushed to put on the CD of 'Mambo No. 5', sung (sic) by Bob the Builder.

Since being introduced to WWF (World Wrestling Federation) at my mother's house, he is now addicted – and I use the word carefully. He lives only for Fridays when Sky Sports One broadcasts two hours of this so-called 'Sports Entertainment'. His heroes are The Rock and The Undertaker, and his antiheroes are Stone Cold Steve Austin and DDP (Diamond Dallas Page). All of the above are hideous-looking, over-muscled brutes who do not look as if they have ever read world literature, and probably think that Nabokov is an illegal steroid.

Last night I found William six inches from the TV watching an action replay of The Rock's finishing manoeuvre. His victim was Booker T. The Rock was smashing Booker T's head through a table. When I made an objection, William said, 'Quiet, Dad. The Rock's going for the one-two-three count. If he gets it, he'll leave the Astrodome with the WWF championship belt.'

I pointed out to William that wrestling was merely a sublimation of sub-erotic activity. The hulks refuse to accept the truth – that they have more in common with Oscar Wilde than they can possibly know. William shouted, 'For God's sake, stop talkin'!' I took the remote from him and flipped through the channels, looking for a David Jason drama. William screamed, then held his breath until his lips turned blue. He only resumed breathing when I flicked back to Sky Sports One.

Sunday, August 26

Pandora claims that she has been approached by the *News Of The World* to visit Jeffrey Archer in prison and acquire, by whatever means, his DNA – £10,000 was mentioned. After some thought, she turned it down.

Saturday, September 1

I am powerless to make my boys either happy or unhappy. External forces dictate their mood. Namely, sport. As Glenn settled down in front of the television with a bag of nachos and a cheese dip to watch Leicestershire play Somerset, in the final of the Cheltenham and Gloucester Trophy at Lord's, he said, 'Don't do no hooverin' in 'ere, Dad, I gotta concentrate on the match.'

I pleaded with him to turn down the sound on the TV and listen to the commentary on Radio 4. I said, 'At least that way you will hear some erudite conversation.' I brought in the Sony portable and switched it on to hear Henry Blofeld and Jonathan Agnew discussing a chocolate cake sent in by a listener, a Mrs Daphne Calf, from Wolverhampton. Then Blofeld said, 'Aggers, my dear old thing, you're looking frightfully smart today.'

Glenn rolled his eyes at William, who grabbed the TV remote and turned up the sound. I took the radio into the kitchen and fiddled with the knob until I found Classic FM. I washed up to the sound of

Gershwin's *Rhapsody In Blue*, which always reminds me of Skegness. It was playing when my father confessed to my mother that he had sired a child by another woman.

As I dried up, I wondered where my half-brother Brett was, and what he was doing. I worked out that he'd be about 19 by now. William came out of the living room during the advert breaks to snatch bits of food and to go to the toilet. But Glenn stayed glued to the TV, groaning and occasionally shouting ferociously at the screen. I heard his cry of despair when Leicestershire lost. I went in to see him and William in tears.

My parents came round later to watch the England–Germany match. When, after six minutes, Germany scored, my father shouted, 'I blame Posh Spice for this. It's her fault Beckham strained his groin. She should be put in purdah before a big match!'

At half-time, in the kitchen, I asked my father about my brother, Brett Mole. He said, 'Not now, Adrian, England are 2–1 up.' At full time, I tried again. But my father was incoherent with xenophobic joy.

Wednesday, September 5
Ashby de la Zouch

It comes as no surprise to me to learn of Iain Duncan Smith's Japanese ancestry. There is the look of the Orient about him. And, when quizzed by John Humphrys, some of his answers were somewhat inscrutable. Perhaps he should fall on his sword, and give old Clarkie a chance. Speaking metaphorically, of course.

I have been preoccupied lately with thoughts about my half-brother, Brett. Where is he? Does he still live with his mother, Doreen Slater, aka Stick Insect? How tall is he? I wish I'd been called Brett, rather than Adrian. Bretts climb mountains, play lead guitar at Wembley Stadium and take beautiful women to bed, etc.

My newly wed parents seem less in love than they did last week. My mother was prescribed new spectacles yesterday, and was able to see my father clearly for the first time in many years. She confessed to me that she was 'gobsmacked' at 'how old your dad looks. What's happened to his face?' She said that he looks like some 'sort of reptile'. I explained to her that during the time he was married to Tania Braithwaite, she had insisted he attend a tanning parlour once a week. My mother snorted contemptuously, and said, 'That's not all she insisted on. He's learned a few tricks in bed that I'm not happy with.'

Thursday, September 6

I have decided to make contact with Brett. So I asked my father to come for afternoon tea. Over cucumber sandwiches and a pot of Earl Grey, I asked him bluntly if he has any contact with his other son. My father avoided the question by complaining about the sandwiches, calling them 'poncy', and the tea, saying it was 'as weak as a sailor's arsehole'. Eventually, he confided to me that he had been sending Doreen Slater £20 a week since Brett's birth. He was glad that Brett had won a scholarship to Balliol College, Oxford, to read English, because it meant him being 20 quid a week better off.

Balliol College, Oxford! How did he do it? His mother was so thick she thought a semi-colon was a partial colostomy. I have written to Brett, care of Balliol College. The formality of a letter is needed, in the circumstances.

Monday, September 10
Ashby de la Zouch

A letter from Oxford! A vellum envelope, addressed to me in exquisite copperplate handwriting. Inside, a matching piece of personalized notepaper, headed Brett Mole, Balliol College, Oxford. Website: www.brettmole.com.

Dear Adrian,
 What a lark. We must meet and swap goss about our mutual father. When are you next in Oxford?
 Yours fraternally,
 Brett

I logged on immediately to www.brettmole and learned more about my half-brother than I needed to know. There were photographs of Brett mountaineering, white-water kayaking, playing tennis, limboing on a Caribbean beach, modelling on a catwalk and shaking hands with Prince Charles. His website informed me that Brett is 6 ft 2 in. tall, takes a 16-inch collar and size 11 shoes.

On another page I discovered that Brett achieved 14 GCSEs at 'A' grade. His four A-levels were starred. He has published a volume of poetry, called *Blow Out*

The Candle. The reviews were ecstatic. I hate him already.

I emailed him the following message: 'Dear Brett, I thank you for your letter of the 10th. Sadly, I am almost never in Oxford. Yours sincerely, Adrian (Mole)'.

Disconcertingly, Brett emailed back almost at once. 'Hi Bro, Leaving soonest for train to Leicester. See you around 4pm today.' I emailed back that I had got the builders in, and that there was no water, heat, light or toilet facilities, and suggested that he postpone his visit for at least six months. I finished with, 'Please confirm that you are not coming.'

I waited by the machine for over half an hour, but no reply came. I am not ashamed of living in a council house on a sink estate. As for graffiti and abandoned cars, I hardly notice them. But Brett almost certainly will. I tidied up as best I could, and rearranged the bookcase so that he could not fail to see that I was conversant with Dostoevsky, Tolstoy and Chekhov. At 4.05 p.m., I heard the taxi pull up outside, then a confident voice boomed, 'Where's my brother?'

Sunday, September 23
Ashby de la Zouch

Brett is still here. He claims that the events of September 11 have traumatized him and have rendered him incapable of using transport of any kind. Over breakfast this morning, he said to me, 'I could be here for ever, Adrian.' He is formidably clever, and seems to have read every book printed in English, French and German since Caxton invented the printing press. Infuriatingly, he quotes from them constantly, and corrects my own attributions.

He has been helping out Glenn with his homework; consequently, the teachers at Neil Armstrong Community College are now talking excitedly about the boy being only the second pupil to get to Oxbridge (the first was Pandora). William is in love with 'Uncle Brett', and follows him around the house like the Old Shep that Elvis sang about. Origami is only one of Brett's many skills. This morning he transformed the G2 section of the *Guardian* into Balliol College, complete with dons and undergraduates.

He is constantly on the phone to his many friends around the world. He assures me that he will stump up for his share of the phone bill. Then, a moment later, laughs about his state of penury.

He and my father get on like a house in flames, and talk endlessly about football players, cricketers and rugby oafs – people I have never heard of.

Monday, September 24

I heard with alarm today that, due to the coming 'Crusade' or 'Infinite Justice' or 'The Conflict' or 'World War Three', David Blunkett has warned that my civil liberties may be restricted in the future, and that I may have to carry an identity card with me at all times. Since I am constantly losing my Sainsbury's Reward Card, the future looks dim for me.

Tuesday, September 25

Brett is making a documentary about post-twin towers trauma using a Panasonic hand-held digital video camera. Channel 4 and BBC2 are bidding for the rights. He interviewed me at length in the kitchen. When he played it back to me, I noticed that my Afghan coat was hanging on the back of the kitchen door. I asked Brett to re-shoot, but he refused, saying that he would not be censored.

Sunday, September 30
Ashby de la Zouch

Brett has written a 1,500-word article for the *Independent*, headed 'The Osama Bin Laden I Knew'. He claims to have first met Bin Laden in the breakfast room of a boarding house in Blackpool. 'I was immediately suspicious of him,' wrote Brett. 'He claimed to have been in England for five years, yet he did not appear to know that pepper was shaken from the pot with the multi-holes. In the bar that night, he ordered a pint of snowball and a packet of pork trotters [sic]. When I commented that snowballs were usually drunk by women, and in much daintier glasses, Bin Laden snarled, "I am a British citizen, I hate slugs, and I visit a garden centre many times a year. Also, I watch the whores of western culture on *EastEnders*." When our landlady failed to bring him a packet of pork trotters, saying, "It's scratchings you want, love, an' we're out of 'em due to swine fever," he went berserk and shouted, "I am a legitimate citizen of this country – here is my passport and my HGV licence."' After I had finished reading the piece, Brett asked me for a critique. I said, 'It is a tissue of lies from beginning to end. It is a well-known fact that Osama bin Laden does not speak English.'

Brett replied airily, 'Our conversations were conducted in Arabic throughout.'

I scoffed, 'Are you claiming that a Blackpool landlady is fluent in Arabic?'

'Yes,' said Brett. 'Her name is Fatima Hardcastle – we do live in a multicultural society now, you know.'

I know Brett is lying, but how can I prove it? I can only pray that the *Independent* throws this piece of fiction back in his face before he brings shame on the Mole dynasty.

Monday, October 1

I have long suspected that my sister Rosie is not my father's child, and that she was sired by Mr Lucas, our next-door neighbour. My theory was confirmed today when my white-faced mother burst into my kitchen and sobbed, 'If they bring in ID cards with DNA profiling, I'm done.'

Tuesday, October 2

I phoned Pandora at the Grand Hotel in Brighton, and urged her to speak against the introduction of ID cards. She barked, 'Clear this line! Don'tcha know there's a war on?' And then she cut me off.

Saturday, October 6
Ashby de la Zouch

Dear diary, my half-brother is still here. God knows, I am the kindest and most tolerant of men, and I am with the Muslims when it comes to extending the hand of hospitality to those seeking sanctuary. But I have to confess that I am irritated beyond endurance by the presence of Brett Mole in my house. I hate him. I have come to dread the sound of his footsteps on the stairs. I cannot bear the way he seems to suck Rice Krispies down his throat. But I am a lone voice. He is loved and admired by everyone I know.

There is a messianic quality about him. Alarmingly, he told me that he intends to start a new political party financed by the Princess Diana Fund. I told him, angrily, that the day after the Parisian tragedy, I had driven to Kensington Gardens and pinned a £10 note to a tree, together with a poem:

> *Oh Diana!*
> Oh Diana! Was a song of my mother's
> youth.
> Sung by Paul Anka,
> who was small and white of tooth.
> The refrain, Oh Diana!
> Beats inside Mum's head
> A blank, a blank, a doo-dah
> That her Diana is dead.

As you may have noticed, diary, I was unable to find suitable rhymes in order to complete the poem satisfactorily. I still can't. I am thinking about contacting Earl Spencer to inform him of Brett's political ambitions.

Wednesday, October 10

A Harrods van delivered Brett's new bed this morning. It took two men all day to install it in the spare bedroom. It has an in-built telescopic television, a CD player and will adjust to 19 positions. I gasped when I saw the invoice: £7,999. Brett said it was a treat to himself; he has been commissioned by Channel 4 to make a documentary on poverty, and is filming it on my council estate. His old mattress joins the other one in the front garden. I am waiting for the council to remove these eyesores.

Thursday, October 11

Brett has scattered the contents of my wheelie-bin in the front garden, and slashed the mattresses with a Stanley knife. He said it would make a great establishing shot for his documentary, now entitled *Weep, England! Weep!*

Sunday, October 14

That monster, Brett, is still living in my house. He is now sharing his electronic Super-Bed with an assortment of slags from the estate. I have provided Glenn and William with earplugs so that their sleep is not disturbed.

Brett's documentary, *Weep, England! Weep!*, is now in production. Many of the interviews are conducted in this house. Cables cover the floors, and most of the doors have been removed to facilitate camera movements. The house is no longer mine. Why don't I tell him to leave? The sad truth is that I am afraid of him. He makes me feel that I am of low class, unattractive and provincial.

Monday, October 15

I came down this morning to find Sandra Alcock sitting at my kitchen table, half-dressed and spitting on to a block of mascara. When I asked her to cover herself up, she grabbed a tea-towel and tucked it between her bra straps. However, I must admit that the sight of Tracy's long legs in white stilettos stimulated my endocrine system, and I had to turn hurriedly towards the sink to hide my sexual excitement. I wonder if Pamela Pigg would be interested in a bout of sexual intercourse? I heard that she and Alan Clarke split, due to a row over globalization. I'll ring her later today.

Tuesday, October 16

I will be meeting up with Pamela after her dog-training class tonight. She sounded delighted to hear from me again, so with a bit of luck it shouldn't take long to get her into bed. And I won't be forced to waste time messing around with meals, and day trips to historical monuments, etc.

Pamela looked charming in the candlelight at the Costa Brava restaurant, and my tortilla and chips were excellent. But I was in bed by 11 p.m. – alone. I am taking her to Belvoir Castle on Friday.

Wednesday, October 17

I was woken by Sandra Alcock at 3.15 a.m. She was standing in my front garden, screaming that Brett Mole was a bastard. And that Justine Turner was a scut-bag. Brett filmed the whole scene, up until the police arrived and took Sandra and Justine away.

Friday, October 19

We explored every corridor of Belvoir Castle. Had scones in the tea room. I even bought Pamela a tea-towel. Yet I slept alone. Why?

Monday, October 22
Ashby de la Zouch

Glenn has been excluded from school, for calling Tony Blair a twat. He brought home a note from Roger Patience, the headmaster, which said:

Dear Mr Mole,

In this time of national crises, it is incumbent on us all to support our government. During a senior pupils' debate, chaired by myself, your son Glenn succeeded in undermining the morale of teachers and pupils alike by his passionate denunciation of the bombing of Afghanistan. He also called our great leader, Mr Blair, 'a leading twat'. I have therefore excluded him from the school premises for the duration of the war.

I hope to God (or Allah) that the war will be over by Christmas. I can't have Glenn hanging around the house all day. It is imperative that I finish my post-twin towers novel quickly. The book (as yet no publisher) must be ready for publication in the spring.

Glenn protested his innocence, saying, 'I didn't say Tony Blair was a leading twat. I said he was leading TWAT (The War Against Terrorism).'

Tuesday, October 23

I went into the chemist this morning to buy a tin of Johnson's baby powder. The shelves where this innocent product is usually kept were bare. The girl behind the counter said, 'It's cos of anthrax.' She informed me, somewhat pompously, that if I wished to purchase talcum powder, I would have to give my name and address, and prove it by showing my last three gas bills. I left the shop in disgust, empty-handed.

Wednesday, October 24

Brett's documentary, *Weep, England! Weep!*, which was meant to expose the wasted lives of sink council estate tenants, has been cancelled by the commissioning editor, who emailed, 'Your doco is not conducive to the national interest at this time.' I am overjoyed to tell you, dear diary, that within the space of two hours, Brett, the crew and the equipment were gone.

Thursday, October 25, 2 a.m.

I have just had a distraught phone call from Pamela Pigg. She told me that her body was covered in red spots: 'It's smallpox!' I drove to her house and examined her naked body. By a process of elimination, I finally deduced that she was allergic to the hyacinth bulbs she'd been potting earlier in the day.

Friday, October 26
Ashby de la Zouch

What's going on? Chaos surrounds me. Has a butterfly flapped its wings in an Amazonian rainforest and dictated how my life is to be? Alan Clarke appeared on my doorstep in the early hours of the morning, sobbing that I had stolen 'the love of his life, Pamela Pigg'.

I led him into the kitchen and listened as he ranted that he'd watched through Pamela's Ikea bamboo blinds, as she stood naked in her bedroom with me. I tried to explain that I was dabbing camomile lotion on to her skin, which was inflamed by hyacinth bulb allergy, but he obviously didn't believe me. Ikea should warn their customers that their bamboo blinds do not guarantee privacy. Clarke rolled a joint and offered me a puff. With Mr Blunkett's permission, I accepted. My head began to spin and I found myself blurting out the plot of my new novel. 'An allegory about twins called Jack and John Towers who are struck down by a fatal illness.' It was dawn before Clarke left.

Saturday, October 27

Mohammed is convinced that oil is at the centre of the Afghan war. He should know, he is the manager of a BP garage and as such has insider knowledge.

Sunday, October 28

The day started well. My mother and father took the boys to Leicester's Golden Mile to watch the Diwali celebrations. With the house empty for once, I phoned Pamela and asked her round for tea. By 4 p.m. we were in bed. There was no sign of the hyacinth allergy. Her skin was pale and smooth. Sexual intercourse was taking place when, at 4.25 p.m., the bed shook. In fact, the whole house shook and several slates fell off the roof. Pamela muttered into my neck, 'My God, Adrian, that's the first time the earth has moved for me.'

Monday, October 29

The headline in the *Leicester Mercury* screamed 'EARTHQUAKE! DID YOU FEEL THE TREMOR?' Apparently, Pamela and I were at the very epicentre of a 3.8 on the Richter scale, which caused terrified residents of Melton Mowbray and North Leicestershire to flee their homes in terror. A box on the front page of the *Mercury* asked its readers, 'What were you doing when the earthquake struck? Let our news desk know.' I hope to God Pamela does not comply with this request.

Monday, November 5
Ashby de la Zouch

My *Independent* was not delivered this morning. I went to the newsagent to complain and collect it in person. A youth of about 14 was sitting on the pavement outside the shop, next to a balloon wrapped in a bundle of rags. The balloon was sporting a crudely felt-tipped beard and round glasses.

As I passed by, the youth muttered, 'Penny for the guy?' I searched through the small change in my wallet and gave him a penny. He dashed it angrily to the ground and said, 'Tight bastard.' I said I had rarely seen such a poor representation of Guy Fawkes. He adjusted the rags on top of the balloon's head and said, 'That's because it ain't Guy Fawkes, it's Osmar bin Laden, ain't it? We're burnin' 'im on the reccy tonight.'

11 p.m.
That's the last back-garden bonfire party I will ever throw. The sausages burst inside the oven, the potatoes burned to cinders and my economy box of fireworks lasted less than 10 minutes. Neither of the Catherine wheels spun. My guests were continually turning their heads eastwards, where rockets from the community bonfire were filling the sky with spectacular patterns and colour.

The recreation ground was thronged with my fellow council tenants and their social workers and probation officers. The community police team was in charge of the fireworks and, in a daring social experiment, Wayne Drabble, the arsonist who burned down the scout hut last year, was in charge of the bonfire. I bumped into Mohammed at the halal barbecue, and he told me that his youngest brother, Imran, is talking hot-headedly of flying to Afghanistan to fight alongside his Islamic brothers.

Mohammed said that Imran had tried to persuade

his girlfriend, Kylie Dodge, to cover herself up with a burka, and walk 10 paces behind him. But she said she had a good pair of legs and she weren't going to cover them up for nobody. Mohammed went on to say that he doubted that Imran could find his way to Heathrow, let alone Afghanistan. He said, 'And he'd have to buy a beard from a joke shop, cos he ain't never needed to shave, not once in his whole life.'

Sunday, November 11
Ashby de la Zouch

As I was making my way to B&Q this morning with William, to buy spare bulbs for our Christmas tree lights, I passed a group of ancient men and women marching towards the war memorial. Some were carrying wreaths of poppies, others had medals pinned to their anoraks.

One old bloke, a double amputee, was being pushed in a wheelchair by his wizened wife. William asked in too loud a voice, 'Where's that man's legs gone, Dad?' I answered, 'He left them in some corner of a foreign field, so that we English could be free men and women, son.'

A Boys Brigade band full of spotty youths began

to play 'Pack Up Your Troubles In Your Old Kitbag'. The old people tried to march in time to the music, but some of them were too slow to keep up. Tears pricked my eyes. I dashed them away as we entered the superstore. As we made our way through to the Christmas department, William asked me if I would have to go to war, to fight 'Osmar' bin Laden. I told him that I was a pacifist and did not believe in war. William said, 'But what if Mr Bin Laden came into my bedroom and was going to kill me. Would you let him, Dad?'

It was a tricky moral dilemma, which was not helped when my mother appeared from behind an artificial conifer, saying, 'Yes, what would you do, Mr bleedin' pacifist?'

I stammered out that in the unlikely circumstance of the world's most wanted terrorist appearing in William's bedroom, then of course I would arm wrestle Bin Laden to the floor and keep him there until help arrived in the form of a panda car from Ashby de la Zouch police headquarters.

William seemed reassured and went off to watch a mechanical Santa ringing a bell. But my mother gave a nasty laugh and said, 'The last time you were in an arm wrestling competition was in 1982, at the youth club table-top sports day. You were beaten 10 times out of 10 by Pandora Braithwaite. You were wearing that brown jumper that Grandma knitted you for your birthday.'

My mother's memory is phenomenal. She could go on stage as Pauline Mole, The Memory Woman.

Wednesday, November 21
Ashby de la Zouch

Mohammed has been arrested! His brother Imran told me that Mohammed had been stacking bags of Real-Wood logs on the forecourt when he was surrounded by police marksmen, who ordered him to take off his clothes and walk towards them with his hands up. Before he got into the back of the van, Mohammed shouted (according to a witness, Wayne Worthington, who had gone to the garage to pick up the wrestling magazine, *Raw*), 'I was only parked on that double yellow for two minutes!' I think it's disgusting that precious police resources are being squandered on minor parking offences.

My allegorical novel, *Jack And John Towers*, is proving difficult to write. Mainly because I have never been to New York. Yet I must press on. Any writer worth his salt has to pen a post-twin towers book. I expect Will Self is writing along similar lines. Note to self (myself): remember to ring the multiplex and book tickets for *Harry Potter*. William has said he will kill himself if he isn't taken to see the film soon.

Thursday, November 22

Imran came round this morning. I offered him a cup of tea and a slice of toast. He shook his head and said, irritably, 'It's Ramadan, Moley. I'm fasting, ain't I?' He came to tell me that his brother has been detained on 'suspicion of terrorism'. Apparently, an anonymous caller had informed the security forces that Mohammed had taken a flying lesson at Leicester airport. Imran said, 'It's all my fault: I bought him a flying lesson gift voucher last Christmas.' I sent a text message to Pandora: 'Our mutual schoolfriend, Mohammed, is a victim of state repression. Ring soonest.'

Friday, November 23

Spent all day on the phone, organizing a 'Free Mohammed' rally in the town hall square. An alliance is forming, which includes BP customers, Nigel's Gays Against Daisy Cutters Group, and Alan Clarke has promised to attend with his Morris Men. No word from Pandora.

The following was found on a scrap of Bronco toilet paper in Adrian's house:

Saturday, November 24, 4 a.m.

A dawn raid! Diaries, computer, mobile phone impounded. Am being arrested under Blunkett's anti-terrorist bill. Please inform Liberty. Where will they take me? And for how long? I'm finished.